LÉO TRÉZENIK

THE CONFESSION
OF A MADMAN

TRANSLATED AND WITH AN INTRODUCTION BY
BRIAN STABLEFORD

THIS IS A SNUGGLY BOOK

ISBN: 978-1-64525-088-3

THE CONFESSION OF A MADMAN

"LÉO TRÉZENIK" was the pseudonym assumed Léo Épinette (1855-1902). He was a French poet, novelist and journalist who, in 1883, co-founded the literary journal *Lutèce*, the first periodical explicitly associated with "Symbolist" poetry, publishing, among many others, the works of Paul Verlaine. Among his works are *Proses décadentes* (1886), *L'abbé Coqueluche* (1889), and *La Confession d'un fou* (1890).

BRIAN STABLEFORD's scholarly work includes *New Atlantis: A Narrative History of Scientific Romance* (Wildside Press, 2016), *The Plurality of Imaginary Worlds: The Evolution of French roman scientifique* (Black Coat Press, 2017) and *Tales of Enchantment and Disenchantment: A History of Faerie* (Black Coat Press, 2019). He has translated more than three hundred volumes from the French, mostly in the genres of *roman scientifique, contes de fées* and Romantic and Symbolist fiction.

His recent fiction includes the visionary science fiction novel *The Revelations of Time and Space* (2020) and its sequel *After the Revelation* (2021); the last in his long series of "Tales of the Genetic Revolution," *The Elusive Shadows* (2020); and the comedy fantasy *Meat on the Bone* (2021), all published by Snuggly Books.

CONTENTS

INTRODUCTION

L A CONFESSION D'UN FOU by "Léo Trézenik"
(Léon-Pierre-Marie Épinette, 1855-1902), here
translated as *The Confession of a Madman*, was originally published by Paul Ollendorff in 1890. It is one
of the most substantial contributions to a subgenre of
Romantic fiction that details delusional fantasies: accounts of strange experiences that could be interpreted
as supernatural hauntings or as symptoms of mental
derangement. Such stories underwent a marked shift
of emphasis during the nineteenth century as pioneers of scientific psychology and neurophysiology
produced more sophisticated accounts of common
phenomena of mental disturbance.

Trézenik's short novel was written at a time when
interest in the observations and theories of the re-
searchers working in the "clinical asylums" of Paris
was intense, particularly among writers, who had
something at stake in the interpretations of their work
offered by scientific investigators, and most particularly of all among writers associated with what came
to be known as the Decadent Movement. Trézenik

had played a significant part in the popularization of that label in his co-editing with Charles Morice of the Symbolist periodical *Lutèce*, in which he reacted against the accusation made by hostile journalists that contemporary poetry was "decadent," rejecting the charge but appropriating the label for his own collection of *Proses décadentes* (1886; tr. as *Decadent Prose Pieces*). As a former medical student he was well-acquainted with the theses regarding the connections between contemporary literature and mental aberration that were being bandied about contemporary Paris and well-placed to react to them in his own literary work. As a neo-Romantic writer and literary theorist, he was also well-aware of the history of previous literary responses to similar arguments, and there was no one better equipped to write a narrative bringing those various threads of thought together in an exemplary fashion.

The great pioneer of Romantic prose fiction, Charles Nodier, took a keen interest in the wellsprings of his own creativity, particularly the phenomena of dreams and hallucinations, and published an important investigative essay, "De Quelque phénomènes du sommeil" (tr. as "On the Phenomena of Sleep") in the *Revue de Paris* in 1831. The giants of the Romantic Movement, including Victor Hugo, Honoré de Balzac and Théophile Gautier—all members of Nodier's *cénacle*—were familiar with his ideas and deployed or varied them in distinctive ways in their own works. They undoubtedly believed, with good reason, that as creative artists they had a better insight into the arcane workings of the human mind than contemporary scientists, many of whom were positivists intent on dismissing the vagaries of subjective experience from the field of reliable knowledge. Romanticism was, by definition, fundamentally opposed to that attempted dismissal, determined to focus on the subjective, if necessary at the expense of the objective, in order to obtain a clearer sight and a better understanding of the way in which human mentality and emotion function.

The writer who borrowed most heavily from Nodier was Gautier, who later became, partly by accident, the great theorist of "Decadent art," in his eulogistic appreciation of the work of Charles Baudelaire. In particular, Gautier penned a classic series of hallucinatory fantasies in which sensitive young men—embodiments of the Romantic ideal—experience supernatural relationships with marvelous females. The relationships sometimes prove fatal, figuratively if not literally, as in "La Morte amoureuse" (1836; tr. as "The Beautiful Revenant" and as "Clarimonde") and "Arria Marcella" (1852), but are necessarily transient in any case, the protagonists either having to come down to earth, as in "Omphale" (1834) and "Le pied de momie" (1840; tr. as *The Mummy's Foot*), or securing a relationship impossible in the real world in a hypothetical afterlife, as in *Spirite* (1865)—but the narratives take it for granted that real life has nothing to offer that can compare with the intensity of the supernatural or hallucinatory relationships. That group of stories is directly ancestral to Trézenik's *La*

9

Confession d'un fou, but whereas Gautier was always willing to accept the supernatural interpretation of his protagonists' experiences, at least as a possibility and sometimes assertively, Trézenik was operating within the context of a different world-view and, as his title suggests, his protagonist rejects supernatural explanations *a priori*—although he is, by definition, an unreliable narrator, and the underlying rhetoric of his narrative is a little more generous, admitting the hypothesis of the succubus, tolerated gladly by Gautier, to the list of possibilities to be entertained only to be sternly rejected.

The underlying rhetoric of Trézenik's story is also more generous in respect of other hypotheses, which were much more fashionable in 1890. Gautier's hallucinatory fantasies also include one that had (and still has) the remarkable distinction of being mistaken for factual reportage, "Le Club des hashischins" (1846; tr. as "The Club of Hashishins"), in which a scientific investigator gathers volunteers to sample hashish in order to investigate their visions. The mistake was easy enough to make, because one of the Parisian pioneers of psychological investigation, Joseph Moreau, who styled himself Moreau de Tours in order to distinguish himself from notable namesakes, really did recruit volunteers to assist him in the research for his study *Du Hachisch et de l'aliénation mentale* (1845), and took care to include writers, probably including Gautier. The visions that Gautier's protagonist experiences in the story are based on the hallucinatory fantasies of E. T. A. Hoffmann, who allegedly obtained his own inspiration from intoxication, and Gautier was inevitably familiar with anecdotes alleging that Humphry Davy had supplied nitrous oxide to various members of the English Romantic Movement as an imaginative aid. We can only speculate as to how much inside information Gautier had about the use of opium by Charles Nodier and other members of the *cénacles*, but there is no doubt that such usage was rife, and it was decisively popularized by Charles Baudelaire, whose investigation of *Les Paradis artificiels* (1860) made a major contribution to the myth that "Le Club des hachischins" was an authentic document. The protagonist of *Le Confession d'un fou* never mentions his own drug use, but the epilogue relating the "factual backcloth" to the delusion is careful to do so, in order to permit the interpretation that the fashionable opiate of the day—morphine—might have made a considerable contribution to the notional narrator's hallucination.

The obliquity of that reference reflects the fact that certain sources of inspiration deliberately employed by Romantic and Decadent writers were, if not entirely unmentionable, more often covert than overt. The exact extent of the contribution made to Romantic literature by laudanum and other psychotropic concoctions is impossible to determine, users generally remaining coy even after the spectacular example set by Thomas De Quncey's notorious *Confessions of an English Opium-Eater* (1821), which was the primary source of Baudelaire's investigations. Nodier once made a similar confession in an attempt to get himself out of trouble, blaming excessive use of opium for a slander aimed at Napoléon that led to his imprisonment, but his principal drug-fueled dream-fantasy, *Histoire du roi de Bohème et ses sept châteaux* (1830; tr. as *The Story of the King of Bohemia and His Seven Castles*) only mentions opium pills once, in passing, by way of a hint. If opium was semi-mentionable within its literary products, however, there were other possible sources of Romantic inspiration that were less so, and even the commentary literature supplied by proto-psychologists was often delicate in expression.

All autobiography is, of course, fiction; it consists of self-serving perversions of actual events intended to justify or magnify the author. Autobiography routinely claims to be revealing the truth—"laying bare the human heart," as one conventional phrase has it—but actually intends to massage the truth by substituting something more palatable. Writers of fictitious autobiographies know that perfectly well, and it adds a crucial extra layer to the rhetoric of their fiction. The ostensible writer of *Le Confession d'un fou* insists that he is writing only for himself, as a kind of self-therapy, and that he therefore feels free to include observations that he would censor from any account intended to be seen by others. That is, of course, a double bluff even within the fictitious manuscript; the supposed "honesty" in trivial matters serves to cover up the fact that more important ones remain almost unmentioned there, only referenced in parenthetical remarks and quotations, deceptively.

12

The biography of the protagonist of the novel is not the biography of the author. It differs therefrom in various conspicuous ways; on the other hand, there are enough points of contact between the two to encourage, if not to compel, the reader to wonder exactly how much of the author's real thinking there might be in the thinking of the protagonist, and to what extent the fictional nature of the text might be used as a cover for expressing opinions and making judgments that could not be expressed on his own behalf for diplomatic reasons. The account of the culmination of the protagonist's delusion is pure fiction, but that does not rule out the possibility that, like his character, Léo Trézenik might occasionally have wondered whether he might be in danger of going mad, or might even be in the process of going mad. Indeed, given the circumstances in which he was writing, it would be astonishing if he had not occasionally entertained that hypothesis, if only to dismiss it as ridiculous—and the same is true of all of his contemporaries, especially those associated with the Decadent Movement, who were routinely accused of insanity by hostile critics. In much the same spirit that they accepted and twisted the charge of "decadence," of course, some of them were not entirely displeased by the questioning of their sanity, and were eager to treat such suspicions as evidence of their genius.

The idea that genius and madness are closely related had been widely entertained at least since Aristotle, but it was dramatically popularized and sophisticated in the nineteenth century, most prominently by the

Italian positivist proto-psychologist Cesare Lombroso in *Genio e follia* (1864; tr. as *Genius and Madness*), who claimed that many, if not all, great geniuses, displayed what he called "degenerative symptoms," detectable in various physical afflictions and measurable in the form of their skulls. In France similar ideas had already been promoted by Louis-François Lélut's *Du démon de Socrates* (1836; reprinted 1856), a pioneering exercise in "retrospective diagnosis," which had little impact at first but increased its influence markedly as the century progressed. Lélut, who supervised the reform of Bicêtre that made it a model for "clinical asylums," and Lombroso, whose pseudoscientific analyses offered methodological inspiration to those seeking to treat their inmates, had a considerable influence on the administrators of such institutions who followed in Lélut's footsteps—including Benjamin Ball, who is specifically cited in Trézenik's story. Writers of neo-Romantic fiction, unsurprisingly, often produced stories asserting and illustrating the opinion that the administrators of clinical asylums were far less sane than their inmates, and that their "treatments" were a species of sadistically motivated torture.[1]

Le Confession d'un fou appeared two years before the most spectacular development of Cesare Lombroso's ideas, *Entartung* (1892-93; tr. as *Degeneration*) written in German by Max Nordau, but based on work done in Paris while Nordau was one of Benjamin Ball's

---

1 cf, for instance, *Les Microbes humains* (1886; tr. as *The Human Microbes*) by Louise Michel and *Le Masque* (1894; tr. as "The Mask") by Gilbert-Augustin Thierry.

fellow students of the most famous of all Parisian clinical psychologists, Jean-Martin Charcot. Like Ball at the Hôpital Sainte-Anne, Charcot gave public lecture-courses at the Salpêtrière, attended by many writers interested in psychological theories; both men undoubtedly had some knowledge of Nordau's ideas while his book was still in the process of gestation, and which were, to some extent "in the air" in Paris in1890. Trézenik, who attended some of Ball's lectures, is therefore likely to have had a peripheral acquaintance with them, or at least with similar theses.

Nordau's assertion, in a nutshell, is that practitioners of "Decadent art" in general, and the precursors and exponents of the Parisian Decadent Movement in particular, were not only symptomatic of but largely responsible for contemporary social decadence, constituting a contagious seed of madness. Charcot—who features in *Entartung* as a horrible example of degeneration—cannot have approved, and Ball might well have been hostile too, as Trézenik must have been, but they could hardly help reacting to the thesis in their various ways. Trézenik, as one of the inventors and popularizers of the paradoxical idea of *fin-de-siècle* Decadent literature, presumably felt compelled to express his reaction in his own sarcastically paradoxical fashion, and *La Confession d'un fou* is the principal component of that reaction, full of subtle and sophisticated literary ambiguity, but possibly reflective of a real anxiety.

The exact nature and configuration of that hypothetical authorial anxiety is necessarily occult and undecipherable; all that the story contains is teasing hints, and it is notable that even the key quotation from Benjamin Ball that it is careful to include is euphemistic, veiling its own brutal implication in a fashion that is as typical of medical jargon as it is of literary artistry. All that the reader can really know is what the narrative actually says; what it might have deliberately left out is purely a matter of guesswork. Every reader is therefore free to adopt an idiosyncratic interpretation of exactly what the madness of the protagonist amounts to, what its real causes might be, and what the precise extent of the author's involvement with his story might have been. The supplementary footnotes that I have added in my capacity as translator might assist speculation, but they are external to the work and it is necessary not to take their implications too seriously, ambiguity and mystification being a fundamental aspect of the artistry of the narrative, and an essential element of the fascination of what is, for the connoisseur of such fictions, a deeply fascinating work.

The translation was made from the copy of the 1890 edition reproduced on the Bibliothèque Nationale's *gallica* website.

—Brian Stableford, April 2020.

THE CONFESSION
OF A MADMAN

To Henry Gauthier-Villars[1]

As people plant an eglantine bush on the thresholds of Norman houses, which grows to frame the doorway and whose dangling flowers and verdure shade and embalm the dwelling, allow me, my dear Henry, to garland the frontispiece of my book with your name, in the hope that the ever-blooming flower of your old amity might cheer up these morose pages.

—Léo Trézenik, January 1890.

---

1 Henry Gauthier-Villars (1859-1931) became notorious in *fin-de-siècle* Paris, in the society of which he was very prominent, as "Willy," the signature he employed on much of his journalistic work and used as a "house-pseudonym" on works he commissioned and edited for the family publishing company, most famously including the classic quasi-autobiographical novels written by his wife, who preferred to sign herself Colette. The next book that Trézenik published after the present one, the story-collection *Histoires normandes*, is by-lined "Léo Trézenik et Willy" and Trézenik's preface asserts that the minority of stories written by his collaborator were planned in concert during the summer of 1890.

In general, every singular state of intelligence ought to be the subject of a monograph, for it is necessary for a clock to go wrong in order to distinguish the counter-weights and mechanisms that we do not notice when the clock is keeping good time.

Taine, Preface to *L'Intelligence*.[1]

1 The historian and sociologist Hippolyte Taine (1828-1893) attempted to produce a scientific analysis of literature, which, along with his other writings, had a considerable influence on many writers of the fin-de-siècle, some of whom—especially his friend Émile Zola—engaged him in fervent debate. *De l'Intelligence* was published in 1870.

PART ONE

I

I sense that I am going mad.

It frightens me to write that sentence; but it is necessary that I get used to fear, since I have just made the decision—the only one that remains to me—to struggle with it hand-to-hand.

I sense that I am going mad!

For more than two years I have been hesitating to formulate that irreparable confession; but today, doubt cannot be put off any longer; the symptoms are getting worse; my only faint hope is in struggle. Perhaps, by force of energy, I can postpone the fatal reckoning . . .

First of all, in order to combat an enemy, it is necessary to recognize that it exists, and afterwards, to make sure of the positions that it occupies.

To recognize that it exists, I have just shown the courage. I have confessed to myself that I felt madness rising within me. Oh, I took a long time to determine myself to make that desperate confession. For two years I have been ingenious in finding all sorts of cowardly explanation that "were not that," and I knew it well. I invented headaches, I alleged overwork, congestive pressures; then, slyly, under the pretext of technical studies, I went to Saint-Anne[1] almost every Sunday morning to compare true madmen, those who are finished, locked up, separated from the rest of society and to compare them with myself. I put their troubled and disequilibrated brains alongside mine in the same balance, my eye glued to the needle; and without admitting to myself that a question had been posed within me, I concluded silently that the advantage was still on my side, since they were mad and did not want to be, whereas I was not yet entirely mad and was still able to note the slightest premonitory symptoms.

It is precisely to conserve that superiority over the madmen of Saint-Anne by confessing my madness— in order to reconnoiter the enemy's positions—that I have decided abruptly to formulate that confession in this journal, where, day by day, I can, so to speak, take the pulse of my brain and register meticulously the smallest progressions of the malady, in spite of the fear that is making my pen tremble in my hand.

I shall proceed with regard to myself like a physician with regard to his patient, searching in my

1 The Hôpital Saint-Anne was originally a farm where inmates from the nearby asylum at Bicêtre were put to work, but it became a "criminal asylum" in its own right in 1863, rebuilt in the context of Baron Haussman's redesigning of Paris. It became a center of intensive medical research and, like the Salpêtrière, opened its doors once a week to visitors, including many *fin-de-siècle* writers, who attended lectures and demonstrations given by its staff.

past life, scrutinizing its antecedents, interrogating heredity in order to exhume from the darkness and distance in which it usually hides the cause of the Evil, assuredly made of a mass of petty reasons, an accumulation of petty motives adding up from year to year to conclude with the present effect. In that fashion I will find the weak point of my organization, the chink in the armor, the precise point at which I have been struck; and perhaps I shall also find the means, if there is still time, if not of stopping the progress of the malady completely, at least of preventing it from galloping.

In addition to the advantage of recognizing and confessing my condition, I have in my favor the privilege of possessing, for the merciless struggle in which I shall necessarily be the victor but which might be prolonged beyond all anticipation, a precious weapon of solid temper and proof against shocks. I am talking about the Will. Intelligence I also have, but it is unsteady, and on some days its acuity weakens; I see things as if through a fog. Well, thanks to my will. I can still—after a painful effort, it is true—blow away that fog and clear my brain of the last wisps that trail here and there. As long as I am in possession of my will, I defy madness to flatten me completely.

Furthermore—I can confess it now that I have entered into the path of confessions—I would have been mad for more than a year, and fit for a straitjacket, without that will. I have had to contend with terrible impulses; there has been an atrocious struggle within me, perhaps only for ten seconds, but of what

27

frightful anguish! If I had not had an energetically tempered soul, I would have lost, and I would have committed the irreparable action that would have given society the right to lock me up. I have resisted; I have struggled; I have been victorious; I have muzzled the strange beast that was growling within me. That day, I understood "possession." Evidently, for ten seconds, I was possessed. By what, or whom? I scarcely dare descend into the dark depths of that question, so fearful am I that the Beast, the Being, the Spirit—the what or whom, in sum—might exist in reality, and simply be dormant within me, and might awaken, and that it might be necessary to enter into combat with it . . . Yes, I am afraid! And yet, I am armed, I know: I have a will that does not bend. There, perhaps, lies salvation.

Physicians have a charming word to designate the nervous, those who are the probable future tenants of Vaucluse or Saint-Anne. They qualify them as "candidates for madness". Let us see, therefore, whether my candidature has been posed by my ascendants, whether they have at least had the amiability of preparing the way for me.

Almost all my relatives are dead, afflicted in the brain.

I was born in a province, at Saint-Roch, in the confines of the Perche and Normandy.

I have often been told in my childhood, in those hours of scutinizing curiosity in which people love to go back into the past to sound the mysteries of genealogy, so full of interest for children, that the grandmother of my grandmother had been the Goddess Reason in 1793.[1] "Oh, but in spite of her," my grandmother protested, with dignity, who told me that as if she were telling me a fairy tale—and it really was a fairy tale for me, that exciting history in which there was even bloodshed—my ancestor having attempt to oppose, weapons in hand, the invasion of her abode by the revolutionary horde.

Goddess Reason! Is it not curious to compare to the ancestral "Goddess Reason" the great-great grandson, a candidate for madness?

The son of the Goddess Reason, my great-grandfather Jean Bardan, died of "excess," according to what I have heard said. "Excess" is scarcely precise; is it a simple provincial metaphor, or a discreet euphemism to veil a fit of madness?

All that I know about him is that, sent one day by his wife to Le Mans to collect a heritage of ten thousand francs, the fellow, instead of returning with his little sum intact, hollowed it out cynically and devoured it to the last écu in company with a dozen local sluts. It was the only feature of the life of that amiable fantasist that the chronicle has been able to tell me.

---

1 La Culte de Raison was established in 1793 as a state-approved atheistic religion by the National Government. It only lasted a year before being abolished by Robespierre, but in that interim it redesignated churches as Temples of Reason, where a great Fête de la Raison was held in Brumaire (in November according to the old calendar), in which a costumed Goddess of Reason played a central role. In Paris the role was played at Notre-Dame by Sophie Momoro; the narrator's grandmother presumably played it in a provincial Temple.

His son, my grandfather, whom my mother did not even know, died very young, leaving my grandmother a widow at twenty-two. He died following an "emotion," laid low in three hours by a cerebral hemorrhage. My grandmother, who adored him, was never consoled. She had what is vulgarly termed "*les sangs tourné?*" What is "curdled blood"? Physicians, instead of explaining the fact, which exists, very nearly deny it by shrugging their shoulders. However, in spite of all negation, my grandmother had "curdled blood." She remained in poor health until the day when, eight or ten years after the death of her husband, she was afflicted by a "black pox," which was suddenly complicated by a fever in the brain—in the brain, I emphasize—which carried her off in forty-eight hours. My mother, Héloïse Barban, was then twelve years old. She was taken in by a distant relative who hastened to marry her off as soon as she was of age.

On my father's side, there is nothing, because nothing is known. I was able, bit by bit, to reconstitute the history of my maternal family, thanks to stories collected here and there from the mouths of a few old inhabitants of the locale who had known it, but my father was from the country, and his family, worn out by laboring the land, is extinct; not one cousin remains.

He must have been orphaned young, I do not know by what causes, and he died before I had the leisure to interrogate him, since that death occurred during my fifteenth year.

It appears that I did not have "two days of life" in me when I was born. My mother refused energetically to allow me to be taken away by a nurse in spite of the insistence of the physician.

"But you don't have two drops of milk, Madame."

My father, an egotist, like the majority of men, redoubted the noise of children and all the inconveniences that are ordinarily the consequence of raising children at home, so he supported him strongly, but my mother held firm. Moreover, she "wore the trousers," because my father, who had acquired the habit early in life of sacrificing everything to his tranquility, left her the exclusive direction of the house without argument.

"The poor child," my mother said, "paltry as he is, won't make old bones with a nurse!"

And I stayed.

II

MY parents were as different physically as they were mentally. My father rather resembled an egg at one end of which short and stout legs emerged, whereas a completely round red head emerged at the other end, without a hint of a beard and with scarcely any hair on his head, which gave him the air of an obese priest in civilian dress. He had heavy eyebrows, a common mouth and a vulgar chin, but his eyes shone with a very bright gleam, which was further augmented when he looked at women—for whom, however, he affected an entirely Biblical scorn.

My father was a bigot; he had a religion composed of a host of petty stupid practices, a whiny religion punctuated with virulent sorties against "the enemies of our holy religion"; he took communion twice a year, with a sanctimonious air, as if overwhelmed by the idea that God was descending into him. He had a blind faith in miracles; the house was full of good blue-and-white Virgins, pink Christs with bloody wounds, pious pictures, little reliquary-frames labeling, under little glass bulbs collared with blue paper, white dusts that the inscriptions declared to be "osseous particles" of Saint Someone-or-Other. In the dark corners of all the corridors, minuscule candles and lanterns burned to either side of a little gilded altar edified on a little shelf. Stitched to his scapular he wore brochettes of medals blessed in all sorts of miraculous chapels,

He did not disdain good cheer, however, and slightly spicy pleasantries between the pear and the cheese, and often invited friends to dinner in order to have a pretext for fortifying the meager quotidian menu seriously.

My mother was a little, dry and rigid woman who never laughed. She had married my father because she had been told that it was *necessary* to marry, and she had accomplished her duty without repugnance, as without enthusiasm, simply because it was *necessary*. She considered amour as something shameful and inadmissible; she called women who lived outside marriage "sluts," while being naïvely astonished that it was possible to find creatures capable of accomplishing, without being forced by the sacrament, what she called—perhaps in memory of the Holy Spirit—the "operation" of marriage. "Those women" had all her scorn and all her disgust.

Naturally, my father and my mother were not "in love"; my mother would have been confused by such a supposition. Perhaps my father . . . but my mother was so scantly a woman, carnally speaking, that my father was obliged to limit himself to the strict execution of his duty. My mother was so "flat" that she wore braces to hold up her skirts, and easily removed her corset without unfastening it by running it over the absence of her hips. It is necessary to say that she was not curvaceous, so little that she was as broad in the waist as the shoulders. Her black dress had two small fan-like gathers that caused an appearance of a bosom to float; but as she was a trifle humpbacked the little gathers almost sagged inwards, with the result that she seemed to have in negative relief what other women possessed in positive relief.

The authors of my days found absolutely nothing in one another that excited them to amour. It is perhaps for that reason that there were never any moments of abandon, tenderness or caressant intimacy between them. Even in bed, my mother never spoke to my father except in the fashion: "Well, Monsieur Daucy . . ."

I never heard my mother name my father, in his presence or in his absence, in any other way than "Monsieur Daucy."

My mother had all the petty qualities of a housewife. She was "orderly" to the point of scrupulousness, and economical—*regardant*, as they say in the region—to the extent of meanness. Although my parents were quite well-to-do, my mother's great preoccupation was saving a few sous on purchases, which she made herself, not wanting to entrust that delicate mission to the maid. She always haggled, no matter what price was proposed; she haggled on principle. Every time she came back from the market she said to my father with satisfaction:

"Guess how much I paid for this rabbit?"

"I don't know—three francs?" my father replied, at random, who did not really care.

And my mother would shrug her shoulders with an expression of commiseration. "Oh, men! this one knows how to buy as I know how to row cabbages. Well, the good woman said thirty-five sous, I offered her twenty-five, and I got it for twenty-seven!"

I am lingering with delight in these memories, in order to persuade myself more firmly that in my mother, at least, there was not the slightest germ of cerebropathy. She had, on the contrary, a calm, pondered intelligence, sagacious with regard to things, full of common sense. She saw life neither in rose nor in black but as it is, in gray. She did not ask of events any more joy than they can furnish, nor of people any more devotion than they can give.

"We aren't put on earth to be happy, but to earn our salvation," she said.

In discussion, she had the most naïve bad faith, never listening to the arguments put forward, for the reason that her interlocutor was always judged in advance, making him right if he was "religious" and wrong if he was impious. Furthermore, she related everything to religion, and her opinions—the few she possessed—had religion for a basis. The virtues that she practiced the least, without a doubt, were Christian charity and humility, because she was so convinced of being eternally in the right when she decided, with religion as a criterion, that "this is good, this is evil; that man is right, the other is wrong." It seems to me that I can still hear her saying, in her curt, somewhat abrupt, tone:

"Oh, Monsieur, I beg your pardon infinitely."

What unctuous irony, imprinted with superior condescension, she put into that adverb, which she pronounced softly, spelling out the syllables—*in-fin-ite-ly*—pinching her thin lips sideways, in a little rictus, impressive for me, accompanied by a slight arrogant blink of her glaucous, coldly staring eyes: a little rictus that persisted on her mouth once the phrase was pronounced, sharpening it further.

My early childhood was sickly and painful. It seemed that life was reluctant to install itself in me. My first sign of existence was a sneeze, but I did not cry, which astonished everyone. The matron that was caring for my mother said rudely that if I did not cry, it was because I did not have the strength. It appears that for two months, when there was mention of me in the quarter, I was called "the little corpse". The gossips always addressed the matron in the same fashion:

"Well, how's the little corpse? What have you done with him?"

In order to bring all the trumps into play, my mother ordered my neck to be circled by a silk ribbon against convulsions, an amber necklace against croup and a scapular from Mont Carmel lined with a Sacred Heart in order to place me under the protection of "Our Lord." Between the scapular and the red flannel of the Sacred Heart, medals of La Délivrande, La Salette, Lourdes, Chartres and Notre-Dame des Victoires were sewn. Finally, my mother declared:

"You know, Monsieur Daucy, I believe that we'd do well, in order to be agreeable to the Holy Virgin, to dedicate Marie-Joseph to her."[1]

"You're right, Madame Daucy," replied my father, simply, as was his habit.

Marie-Joseph! That name was the nightmare of my adolescence. Perhaps the silk ribbon preserved me from convulsions and the amber necklace from croup, but in the cluster of profane or religious amulets that tinkled around my neck the one that ought to protect me from being nervous was certainly forgotten. For I was, and immediately, incurably nervous.

That nervousness had a particular character. It was more an exaltation of sensibility than the clenching, grating and grimacing nervousness customary to the majority of children. My neuropathy was manifest in the form of sudden and irresistible crises of tears in certain particular cases, well-determined and always the same. Strident noises exasperated me; grave and languid noises, the sad airs of the violin and the flute, made me weep. Nevertheless, my crises of tears had two principal causes. The first was the ululation, in winter, of the wind under the doors. As soon as I heard the *vouvououou* of a squall I elongated my little beak in a tearful moue, seemingly asking for mercy and begging the wind to silence its melancholy music; and as the *vouvououou* accentuated, the moue elongated further and a deluge of tears sprang from my

---

1 As noted in the introduction, the author's forenames were Léon-Pierre-Marie.

eyelids, which closed in terror. It was necessary to fit all the doors and all the windows in the house with draught-excluders.

That great sadness, drowned in tears, suddenly broke into hectic sobs when my gaze encountered, on clear nights, the opaline globe of the moon floating in the blue spaces. That fear of the moon gripped me for a long time, and even today, I prefer not to look at the sly face that smiles obliquely on tranquil and silent nights.

Until the age of seven I endured the odious torture of being dressed, implacably, entirely in white. Entirely! A child has a horror of anything that singularizes him; his timidity is alarmed by anything that designates him to the gaze. To be like others, to be made like others, is his great preoccupation; the attraction of the example is irresistible in him. If he protests so violently against an injustice, it is because he sees himself the object of a special measure, and that is so true that he resents a person who punishes him much less than a person who punishes him for a fault that another was able to commit with impunity.

There are children whose soul has been irredeemably ulcerated because, placed by their parents in a school above their status, they find themselves less well-dressed than the others. The uniform in usage in colleges is an excellent thing, because it effaces distances.

Until the age of seven, I always had the appearance of going forth in disguise. Numerous cretins refuse children the right to think before that age, which is the age of reason for the Church. I shall not ask whether a child is responsible for his actions before the age of seven, but what I am sure of is that well before the age of seven a child feels, compares and suffers. And I suffered. I suffered from never having done anything like others, from never having little comrades like others, from not being able to go into the street like others, from the fact that my mother would not let me play like the others, from having her shrill voice suddenly yap, when I succeeded in escaping:

"Oh, my God, what a state you're in, a robe all white this morning. And stockings full of mud! Oh, Marie-Joseph, wretched child, you'll make me die of chagrin!"

And then, in order to have one argument more, an irresistible argument, she scraped my forehead with a long thin finger and cried:

"Oh my God, my God! Look, Monsieur Daucy, he's *swimming*."

"Yes, Marie-Joseph, you're swimming," my father said, placidly. "Come on, sit down there in order to cool down a little."

Furthermore, I always came back from the street very upset. The others were reluctant to admit me to their games.

"Oh, but if your skirts are crumpled, your mother will shout."

My skirts! How dolorously that sounded in my ears. And how conscious I was of the stupid stain that those skirts made, in the dark swarm of the other children!

There was even one of them who replied to me cruelly one day: "And anyway, girls don't come to play with boys."

A girl! Yes, I was a girl. I had skirts like a girl! I was called Marie, like a girl!

I wept for a long time that day, and my tears were very bitter. It was my first big chagrin. And I can confess, since this confession is for me alone, that the wound it inflicted on my self-esteem, now scarred over, sometimes gives me dolorous twinges when my finger touches it.

III

I have noticed that when competent persons ask one another the question, having looked at it from all sides: "Should a child be placed in a boarding-school or take courses externally?" there are always two responses, contradictory and equally affirmative.

"Yes," say some, "it's *necessary* to send him; boarding is necessary to the formation of intelligence, and above all of character; a child has need of the friction of others."

"No," say others, "if you can, keep your child at home. Nothing is worth more than the education of the family. Boarding is uniformity in respect of costume and also uniformity in mentality; you will almost certainly cut your child off from his origins and risk losing him."

The *necessary* of the former answer reminds me analogically, I don't know why, of the: "rabbits require to be skinned alive," of the *Cuisinière bourgeoise*.

But I shall not take a side in the quarrel; it is not a thesis that I am sustaining here, since it is a confession that I am making to myself, and a simple medical observation that I intend to carry through to a conclusion. Let us therefore limit ourselves to what I, personally, gained or lost.

I absolve my parents for having put me in a boarding-school, but I do not thank them for it. I absolve them because it was my interest that they had in mind, with the best faith in the world. And who, without having suffered a great deal, can divine whether any new idea that enters your head will later be a cause of suffering?[1]

In a province, among the three aristocracies—that of birth, that of money and that of education—it is perhaps the last for which people have the greatest attraction or consideration. It is true that the province has a little, for that of birth, of the scorn that the fox in the fable has for the "sour" grapes.

Provincials sometimes end up arriving in the aristocracy of money, although it is more likely to be by virtue of ferocious economy than by labor or speculation; and their vanity wishes for their sons the aristocracy of education, many because it is the only one to which they can aspire, and many also because they are sagely persuaded that money only leads anywhere when it has education for a traveling companion.

My parents lived in Saint-Roch, a little canton of Haut-Perche,[2] privileged, by chance, with an excellent

---

1 The author was placed in the Jesuit college of Saint-François Xavier at Vannes, after which he went on to study medicine at the University of Caen in 1875-76, although his studies were interrupted when his family moved to Paris.
2 There is no canton of Saint-Roch in the Haut-Perche, although

primary school. I was able to make good studies there in French, but Latin was not taught, and my father was very keen that I should do what he called "my humanities."

"You see, Madame Daucy, that one gets nowhere at present without Latin. Marie-Joseph is intelligent, he learns easily, he might perhaps make a doctor."

Never, until that day, had my father given his advice first. My mother was so stupefied that she did not even think of arguing. And it was decided that I would be a doctor. From then on, I was no longer called anything but "Doctor," with emphasis and ostentation.

"So, Doctor! Don't bite your fingernails, Doctor!"

The gossips traded the news with forceful commentaries.

"Oh, don't you know? Little Daucy is going to be a doctor."

"A doctor!"

"Yes, a doctor! His mother is so happy!"

More importance was attached there than in the country, at present, to children who "took the estate of their father," furnishing principally, as an example, wig-makers. All the wig-makers for ten leagues around came from the chief place of the canton. Saint-Roch could not furnish individuals more outstanding.

---

it is a very common name in other regions. The author was born in Rémalard, some twenty kilometres south-east of Montagne-au-Perche. Octave Mirbeau, seven years older than Trézenik, grew up in the town, and the two had a very fractious relationship while living in Paris, continually sniping at one another in their journalistic works; Mirbeau preceded Trézenik to the Jesuit college at Vannes, but was expelled before the latter arrived.

And now, it was about to have a *doctor!*

The schoolmaster, when consulted, affirmed that it was not temeritous to direct me toward such a high destiny. He said to my father: "The lad has good legs; he'll go far."

The deacon of Saint-Roch was therefore charged with "starting me off" in Latin.

Parents are always mistaken when they are ambitious, on behalf of their progeniture, for a situation superior to their own. To remain in one's milieu is the commencement of wisdom; if all sons did what their fathers did, there would be far fewer displaced individuals. The disequilibrium of society would not be produced, plethoric on one side and anemic on the other, of which the logical and unavoidable consequence will be the death of the old world. The source of the evil is at the very bottom, in the foundations. Displacement, flotation, attempts to climb above those fundamental strata, compromise the equilibrium of the entire edifice. Its collapse is no longer anything but a matter of hours. The slightest gust of wind in the summits will cast the whole thing down.

Thus if I, like my father, had sold to the bourgeois of Saint-Roch and the surrounding area, services in *terre de fer*[1] and mantelpiece ornaments, orange-blossom wreaths under glass and wedding-presents, I would now be the securely-placed husband of some fat provincial simpleton devoid of intelligence but devoid of malice, who would heap me with little

---

1 *Terre de fer* was a trade name applied to a species of cheap ceramic imitative of porcelain.

delicacies and progeniture; I would know nothing of Bourget[1] or any psychologists; I would subscribe, like my father, to the *Petit Moniteur*; I would know that when the sky is red it is a sign of rain and that when it is dappled it is, "like a painted whore," of short duration . . . but I would not be in the process of packing my valise for Saint-Anne . . .

The priest who gave me my first lessons in Latin, Abbé Desmares, had obtained as a favor from the bishop permission never to quit Saint-Roch; he stank abominably of rancid fat, tobacco and dirt. His ground-floor room, to which I came to take a lesson twice a day, was illuminated by a window and a glazed door overlooking the garden of the presbytery. His bed, along with an immense wardrobe, occupied the rear. He remained in Saint-Roch for some forty years. In forty years the presbytery's aged maid did not enter his lair once. He made his bed himself when the sheets were changed, about six times a year; he did not want anyone to touch any of his trinkets or any of his furniture, especially his chairs, which were all laden with old books. For forty years the abbé did not permit a thrust of the broom or a flick of the duster; when he picked up a book he tapped the boards with

---

1 Paul Bourget, author of *Essais de psychologie contemporain* (1883), a series of studies of eminent writers from a psychological viewpoint. A great admirer of Hippolyte Taine, Bourget subsequently became the chief exemplar of a school of neo-Naturalist fiction that replaced Émile Zola's fascination with hereditary degeneracy with a more intense focus on the vagaries of individual psychology, of which the present text is an exaggerated and subtly parodic example.

his hand in order to cause the dust to fly away and blew on the edges, that was all.

One day, when I wiped the marble of a chest of drawers discreetly with my finger in order to place my hat on it, he suddenly started coughing a dry and mocking laughter, which contracted his fat little face comically, hollowing out profound wrinkles, and he said to me, while stuffing his nostrils violently with snuff:

"Dust obfuscates, child. *Memento*, however, *quia pulvis es, et in pulverem reverteris.*[1] The Latin is bad; I do not engage you to employ that form in your essays—*Memento quia*—but the advice is good. It's the spirit that it's necessary to see, and not the letter. 'The spirit vivifies, the letter kills.' In that regard, you might tell me that dust is all right, but what about bugs? To which I reply *illico* that your complaint is unfounded; those charming little beasts of the good God nest in the wood of my bed, respectful of my old skin; they rarely venture as far as the window . . ."

He sniffed a further pinch noisily, and continued:

"The psalmist says that the commencement of wisdom is the fear of the Lord, *Initium sapientiae timor Domini.* To commence with, that is very just, but child, to continue to be wise it's necessary to fear women. If, later, you don't succeed in protecting yourself from women, you're doomed. Woman is Eve, the Apple and the Serpent all rolled into one. It's necessary to bar your door to her, and raise an insurmountable barrier between her and you. But for that, it isn't you

---

1 *Memento, homo, quia pulvis es, et in pulverem reverteris* [Remember, man, dust thou art and to dust that shalt revert] is a passage in *Genesis* 3:19 of the Vulgate Bible.

that it's necessary to disgust with her—that might be beyond your strength—it's her that it's necessary to disgust with you. Remember what I'm saying; perhaps you'll understand later. *Cave mulierem.*"

In fact, I have remembered, and have understood.

In the meantime, I swallowed my nausea for two years, and those two years were as dolorous and oppressive for me as two years of nightmare.

Moreover, I am not speaking figuratively.

Among the volumes that lay here and there, in crumbling piles, under verandas of spider-webs, my curiosity, awakened by the rather ragged illuminations of the cover, had spotted a strange book, which I was finally able to leaf through briefly during a brief absence of the priest, and then read at my leisure by introducing myself into his room in the hours when I knew that he was absent.

For me it was a book as revelatory as it was troubling, even though the road followed to arrive at a glimmer of truth was improbably winding. It was a treatise on "demonic possession," with many details regarding incubi and succubi. I was irremediably disturbed by that reading, which frightened me, but in the fascinating horror of which I found an irresistible attraction. The book was illustrated with sketches that clarified luminously the obscurities that the text could still offer to my ignorance.

"Since Marie-Joseph has commenced Latin," my father sagaciously remarked one day, "have you noticed, Madame Daucy, that he is no longer the same? He is now serious and reflective. I believe that we'll make something of him."

IV

I was, in fact, no longer the same. Every night, now, I had nightmares. I suddenly uttered horrible screams that woke the whole house, and when my father arrived at my bedside he found me sitting up in bed, my eyes haggard and my hair stuck to my forehead by a cold sweat that rolled down my cheeks in enormous drops, and I showed him, breathless and my voice hoarse with terror, a horned devil armed with a trident who was floating above my bed, menacing me with his fork . . . When the candles were lit I could still see him, and sometimes, after half an hour of vain attempts to reassure me, my father was obliged to carry me to his bed in order for the vision to fade away. It disappeared as soon as I was out of the room.

Then the nightmares died down. There was a period of calm, but very brief. My cerebral disturbance—of which madness had to be the eventual terminus—was about to take another form.

My bedroom opened on to the first floor landing, directly opposite the well of the staircase; to the left was my parents' bedroom, to the right the black hole of a long corridor leading to storerooms. The staircase was illuminated by a window in a door that opened into the shop, and as my bed was against the wall, directly opposite my door, always open because of my nightmares, whenever my eyes opened in the evening after I had blown out my candle, my gaze wandered in the luminous rectangle that cut across the well of the staircase at an angle, while my parents remained at the little glazed counter of the shop, making up their accounts, until midnight.

One evening, I had only just gone to sleep when I was woken up by a strange feeling of malaise; I had a hollow in my stomach like the impression of suffocation produced by an animal, as if a small cat had fallen asleep curled up on my breast. I put my hand out hesitantly, apprehensive of finding an unknown animal there—we did not possess a cat—but my hand did not encounter anything. However, I had opened my eyes, distressed by the oppression, which was rising from my breast to my throat and almost cutting off my respiration. Suddenly, from the black hole of the corridor, I saw an arm spring forth, agitating a long bony hand with pointed fingers; immediately, as if responding to that signal, a black silhouette emerged from my parents' bedroom, slightly curbed, as if trying to muffle the sound of his footsteps; then two other individuals appeared on the landing, and all four of them disappeared in the corridor. All that was just clear enough for me to be sure of seeing them, but not enough to determine exactly what kind of beings—ghosts or thieves—I was dealing with. Nevertheless, the idea that they might be thieves occurred to me immediately and I uttered a strident cry, which caused my father and my mother to come running. My father made a semblance of inspecting the corridor and the lofts in order to reassure me, while my mother repeated incessantly:

"Come on, go to sleep, child, you're having a dream; it's a nightmare."

I begged them to leave me a candle, quite certain of having *seen*, and I wore myself out reading until dawn; then I went to sleep.

From that moment on until the day that I departed for the college—which is to say, for a year—I had hallucinations almost every night. Careless, or lacking intelligence—or considering the recitation of my fears to be exaggerated—it did not occur to my parents to try, in order to cure me, two simple means: changing my bedroom or leaving me a nightlight. I wallowed—I can find no other expression to render my thought—I wallowed in terror for an entire year, getting up very pale from those haggard nights when, in order to hide from the inevitable panics of daily hallucination, I read stupid novels until dawn, which occupied my imagination while, alas, furnishing it with stupid and false ideas about life, people and things.

Sometimes, surprising the light of my candle, which filtered under his door, my father got up in order to extinguish my light authoritatively, while grumbling, in the presence of a timid objection on my part: "Get away! Is one afraid at your age, great fool." And when, plunged again into opaque darkness, I heard my father make his bed creak by climbing back into it, I was seized, almost at the same instant, by my customary nightmares, my room was instantly populated by invisible beings that I could no longer see, since the luminous frame of the stairway was extinct, but which I could hear agitating, walking, fluttering and whispering around me. My mattress was impacted by sonorous shocks—which were nothing, I realize today, but the galloping palpitations of my heart and my arteries—and murmurs traversed the air, assuredly the buzz of the wings of some moth bewildered by the abrupt disappearance of the light; and under my bed, in the depths of which fear curled me up with the sheets over my head in order no longer to hear the darkness animated, I nevertheless perceived distinctly enormous sighs that resembled the lamentations of an animal in pain, which I attributed to the invisible and impalpable cat that sometimes came during my slumber to sleep on my breast . . .

Today, of course, when I reason, I can find natural causes for all of that, but then I was absolutely convinced that those visions were realities and that my bedroom was haunted. Above all, I remained obstinately convinced of that after one night when my mother heard as I did. That evening, by reason of fatigue, she had gone to bed before my father and she had left her door open as well as mine in order to prevent me from "killing myself reading," as she put it. It was only a quarter of an hour after I had gone to bed when I heard the curt voice of my mother order:

"Marie-Joseph, kill your candle!"

"But Maman . . . !"

"Kill your candle, I tell you! It's time to go to sleep."

"I obeyed, and closed my eyes very quickly, shivering with apprehension; but involuntarily, I opened them a few seconds later. And immediately, I saw the arm emerge from the corridor and summon the others to the customary infernal saraband. The four were soon united on the landing and they started to dance, as usual, making grand gestures; they danced so boldly that suddenly, the staircase began to creak. That creak resounded like a pistol shot in the silence—a pistol shot whose bullet had been fired at me, one might have thought, since I felt a violent shock in the stomach.

"What are you doing, Marie-Joseph?" my mother demanded, abruptly. "Are you out of bed?

I was breathless, and could not articulate a word for several seconds, my lungs gripped by the claw of an anguish so intense that I thought I was going to choke . . .

So my mother *had heard* . . . !"

Her grumpy voice went on: "Reply then! What are you doing walking around like that?"

I finally replied, in a moribund voice: "It isn't me, Maman; it's *them*."

Them, for me, said it all. My mother didn't understand, but she understood, at least, judging by my voice, that I seemed to be in my bed. She had, moreover, struck a match and she came to see for herself that I was lying down and that my teeth were chattering with fear. Then she tried to explain to me that it was nothing; the staircase had creaked, that was all. She had not realized immediately that it had woken her up with a start; that is why she had called out to me. I obtained permission nevertheless to keep my candle illuminated, while promising to try to sleep; my father would extinguish it when he came up.

From that day on I persisted stubbornly in the belief that my bedroom was haunted.

It is only recently that I have found an explanation for that creak heard simultaneously by my mother and myself, a phenomenon that preoccupied me for a long time as a hallucinatory problem whose solution remained undiscoverable, although its elucidation was imperiously indispensable to the health of my tottering reason.

I have reflected a great deal since then on the mysterious phenomena of dreams, of which a good number of authors have given quite plausible explanations.[1]

The hypnotic state is a slumber produced by an external cause, variable in accordance with subjects, and during which one either dreams with open eyes or is the victim of hallucinations provoked by a will superior to yours, by which the subject is duped all the more easily because the faculty of control as in a natural dream, is absent. The subject, on awaken-

---

1 The weekly lectures given at the clinical asylums of Paris during the 1880s included a famous series given at the Salpêtrière by Jean-Martin Charcot detailing his work on the phenomena of hypnosis, and its connection with the phenomena of sleep, including somnambulism; writers of Romantic fiction were already familiar with the intellectual terrain, thanks to Charles Nodier's oft-reprinted seminal essay of 1831.

ing, accomplishes an order given during sleep by the suggester, with less suspicion because that order has been intimated to him in the absence of the faculty of control, and which, in consequence, he mistakes for a spontaneous volition; he does not, therefore, have any thought of disputing the act that he is about to commit; he would dispute it if he could suspect that it had been inspired in him, but, convinced that he wants it naturally, he accomplishes it naturally.

An unprovoked hallucination is an internal sensation; it is a dream formed with the eyes open; the brain creates that sensation in its entirety, as the retina creates entirely when excited by the light of phosphenes. All sensation is the complex result of three actions: the external impression, the transmission to the brain and the internal impression operated by the brain. A hallucination is a sensation deprived of impression and transmission, born within the brain; but as the brain cannot conceive of any perception that is unsupported by an external impression, in the case of hallucination it supposes one, and acts as if the supposition were a reality.

In other terms, a hallucination is an effect without a cause, which judgment declares to be absurd. That is why the latter is induced to conclude that, since there is an effect—the internal image painted on the retina—there must be a cause: an exterior object or being, the point of departure of the image. It is for that reason that sensibility and imagination, in connivance with logic, are induced to conclude the reality of the vision. It is only later, when one has made the education of the brain, that one can affirm, with the aid of reasoning, that what one sees does not exist.

In a dream, what one takes for a conclusion, or a "curious coincidence," is nothing but the determining cause of the dream. It happens to everyone to dream, for example, having been in the Chambre after all sorts of logically connected peregrinations having occurred in one day, to have witnessed the successive entry of all the députés and finally to have seen the session ended by the ringing of the president's bell. At that very moment, you were woken up by the postman ringing the doorbell, which coincided exactly with the president of the Chambre ringing his bell. Now, it is precisely the postman ringing the doorbell that, in the moment preceding your awakening, determined your dream. The brain, in the dream state, as if to release the waking state, functions *in reverse* with a rapidity immeasurably superior to that of the waking state. It folds up, so to speak, and reposes, rather like a waltzer who, after having turned for a long time in one direction, turns in an inverse direction in order to restore his equilibrium.

A hallucination, being a waking dream, has a mechanism analogous to that of a dream. In the case that occupies me, it is, therefore, the creak of the staircase that had determined the hallucination of my predisposed brain, overexcited by expectation, and fully prepared by the prior certainty that I was about to have my vision.

The apparent strangeness, the troubling inexplicability of that coincidence, preoccupied me for a long time. The explanation appeared to me with a limpid evidence, but at the end of how many years of reflection and anxious meditation! Today, possessed by other fears, differently founded, I smile at those infantile terrors, but in that epoch I believed my eyes more than my reason, and, above all, more than the negations of my parents. I considered my bedroom to be inhabited by spirits; I was breathless there every night, in the cold sweat of Fear, and when the day came to depart for the college I was dominated by one unique thought: finally, I would no longer have to go to bed in that room!

And it was, if not with joy, at least with an un-translatable sentiment of relief and deliverance, that I embarked, accompanied by my father, for the un-known country of the boarding-school.

V

I had been at the college for exactly a year—which is to say that I had just entered my fifteenth year—when my father died. If these notes were destined for publicity, there are many things that I would not say. And what I would commence by not mentioning is the impression made on me by my father's death. In order to explain it to myself, to excuse it and exculpate me in my own eyes, I need to recall the extent to which that year of separation, only interrupted by the Easter vacation, after an absence from the paternal house of seven months, had modified me and overturned me from top to bottom.

First of all, this question poses itself in my mind: "In general, do children love their parents?" I know, of course, that for the majority of my fellow citizens, who have vegetated since the beginning of the world on a common foundation of conventional ideas declared to be fundamental Truths, to pose the question is to answer it—in the affirmative. But I also know that if one takes the trouble to descend into the depths of all human affections, it is egotism that one encounters there. That egotism dissimulates itself adroitly in the affection of grown-ups who have gradually learned the necessity of dissimulation, but in children, egotism flourishes entirely at its ease, without any hindrance by adaptation of their naïve little faces to the social mask that is sometimes called politeness, sometimes propriety, respect or consideration, etc.

Children are simply and frankly egotists. Thus, they do not love their parents, in the sense that I, at least, give to the word *love*. They need them, and they lavish caresses and kisses on them in order to get what they covet: treats, toys or sweets. They do not have a single disinterested impulse—which is to say, one that is not thanks for something given or a preliminary flattery in view of something to obtain. Perhaps one loves one's parents later, retrospectively, in memory of the generosity they have had for you. But again, is it good natures and tender ones that lie in wait for cerebral softening?

My own madness will not have cerebral softening as its terminal stage. I have a dry nature. I have sometimes wept with rage, but never from chagrin.

I did not love my parents, but—how shall I put it?—I was used to them. While still young I always had a keen sentiment of the ridiculous; I always held against my father his grotesque belly, and against my mother that she kept me sequestered for seven years under the pretext of white robes. I did not love them; I looked at them askance, but I accepted it. Not entirely, however. Thus, I was never able to habituate myself to the urgent mania that my mother had for mopping me with her saliva when I got my face dirty during the day. I still have in memory the odor, simultaneously acrid and insipid, that sickened me every time, and against which I dared not protest.

What suffered most in me, in my youth, was my self-esteem. Thus, I experienced surges of childish vanity from time to time when I surprised, behind the back of my father and mother going solemnly to high mass, the sniggers and mocking whispers that their compassed stride and my mother's improbably decorated shawls provoked along the road to the church. But in the end, I gradually resigned myself to it.

Then, abruptly, I was put in boarding-school; I went seven months without seeing them. What happened within me during those seven months? Whether the soul of a child, in a certain epoch, is comparable to a wax candle that allows itself to be kneaded, and which not only loses its primitive form but even the memory of what it has been, I cannot say. Those seven months remained very vague in my memory. I recall nothing, absolutely nothing: no precise detail, no vivid emotion.

That entry into a new life must have struck me by its very novelty; but nothing remains of it. I only remember being teased because of my forename, which was very painful. All the rest is, so to speak, drowned in an opaque mist in which the silhouette of no event is visible. I can examine my memory from all angles, to no avail; I see my thought floating inertly in the fog. Only, a week before the vacation, I remember the voice of a fellow student who showed me a little calendar with all the days crossed out since the beginning of the year, and said to me:

"Only one more week, eh? Nice! A hundred and eighty hours!"[1]

And I thought, very placidly, without the slightest glimmer of joy: *Oh, that's right, in a week I'll see Saint-Roch again.*

My father was waiting for me at the railway station, situated two leagues from Saint-Roch, with a carriage. As the weather was fine, my mother had accompanied him. I remember very well both them, as the train arrived, leaning on their elbows, their arms dangling between the points of the little brown barrier, my father with his silk cap, whose tilted peak almost hid one eye, and my mother with her linen bonnet whose heavy strings made a rigid knot directly under her chin, which further exaggerated her stiff appearance. They perceived me in the carriage and waved at me wildly.

"Those are your parents, those old folk?" said a comrade who was continuing a few leagues further on, with a laugh that vexed me horribly.

I hesitated for two seconds, and then I replied, with a disengaged expression, giving him a farewell handshake: "That's the cook and my father's chief clerk."

I had, moreover, no effusion with my parents. I felt icy, as if there were something irreparable between

---

1 The calculation is not incorrect, deriving from the manner in which the French calculated the beginning and end of a week [*huit jours* in French] and the beginning and end of a day at the time when the novel was written.

us. What there was, were those seven months of separation. On seeing them again I did not experience the slightest emotion. Yes, they really were the cook and my father's chief clerk. Or rather, I had—I remember the phenomenon clearly, which surprised me—the sensation of visiting the home of strangers. I felt like an orphan, incomprehensible as that might seem.

It also appeared to me that I had been transported into a dream-land, into the midst of people I did not know, who did not resemble me and who did not speak the same language as me. That impression of living in a dream I have experienced since, but never with the same intensity; that is perhaps because it was entirely new.

It is in details that my sensations of that epoch return to me. I have no vision of the ensemble, and the lines of my memory are troubled, like a photograph of a site that has shifted before the objective lens.

At the college it was customary, when the domestics in the refectory served us cracked plates, to break them on the edge of the table. The day after my arrival on vacation, at breakfast, the maid set before me a plate soiled by a gray crack that might have been several years old. There were a dozen like that which were kept "for use when it was just us." It required *tours de force* every day in order to warm them without breaking them definitively. I took that one in a casual manner and—*snap!*—broke it in two, as at school, on the edge of the table. My parents looked at one another, mute with amazement.

"Are you mad, Marie-Joseph?" my father demanded.

My mother did not say anything; she pinched her thin anemic lips and carefully put aside the two pieces, in order to reunite them with the aid of two clips and some glue.

We had a fortnight of vacation; it was a fortnight of profound ennui. I had no comrade, and apart from one or two visits to Abbé Desmares my sole distraction was walking along the roads with my father. We did not say a word, having rapidly exhausted on the first day all the subjects of conversation in which we could share. Then too, my self-esteem was continually irritated by my father's common and awkward manners and the faults of language that he committed in every sentence. For example, he said "I have" when he should have said "I am," he pronounced *potography*, and referred to a child died of *group* and the *segretary* of the Mairie.

I had attempted several times to correct him, but his routine prevailed over my efforts.

Then too, his homely piety exasperated me, producing an extraordinary refrigeration of my initial fervor. Now my parents told their rosaries every evening in bed, aloud, responding to one another. As soon as the candle was extinct I heard the grave voice of my father commence, in a solemn fashion: "I believe in the Lorrrd, the Almighty Fatherrr . . . and then interminable salutations to Marie; and my mother yapping in her shrill voice. "Hail Mary, Mother of God . . . ," and I went to sleep lulled by the drone of the two voices, the murmur of which rose and fell alternately in the darkness, increasingly indistinct to my ears.

VI

I had been back at the college for about two months, delighted that my vacation was over, when one evening, a prefect of studies summoned me and said, sententiously:

"Your father is very ill, my boy; you have to go, your mother is asking for you."

The idea did not occur to me that my father could die. Furthermore, it was not in the direction of Saint-Roch that my thought went. I saw only one thing in that departure, which was that it coincided precisely with the "prize compositions." And in the train, during the tedium of the journey, I calculated all my chances. I was certain of a prize in Latin translation, a prize in history and an honorable mention in Greek translation . . . And the stations filed past, people encumbered by luggage climbed in and sat down, others got down. The rhythmic noise of the train beat time to a tune in my head, of which I could not rid myself.

At the station at Condé, which served Saint-Roch, I found Mercier, a hirer of carriages that my father employed frequently to ferry his goods. He was waiting for me with a tilbury, and immediately, with a pitying expression that twisted his ferrety features comically, he said to me: "Poor Monsieur Daucy is very ill . . . oh, he's very ill."

Then, seeing that I took the news rather callously, without responding with the conventional deluge of tears that he expected, he started to chat, mingling his loquacity with energetic admonitions to his horse, which he called P'tinoué—*Petit noir*. I was not listening, thinking above all about the prize for Latin translation that I was going to miss. However, a singular word that returned to his mouth repeatedly ended up catching my attention, and I asked him:

"What's this bolide that you're talking about?"

"Yes indeed, a bolide; poor Monsieur Daucy was struck by a bolide."

I started. "Struck by a bolide! What are you telling me, Mercier?"

"Well, it's the physician who said it; it threw him in his garden . . . it's really a bolide, see."

"But how big was this bolide?" I demanded.

"Big," said Mercier, who seemed nonplussed, "but Monsieur Marie-Joseph, one can't see it, since it's in the head, you see."

I could not understand: a bolide in the head. I was ignorant then of "cerebral embolism," the catch-all diagnosis of physicians who want to inform a family in an indecipherable case. And my intellect worked, quite lucidly, arguing with itself, preoccupied by that strange bolide, while my consciousness was numbed as if paralyzed in a sort of lethargy that immobilized me in a fixed attitude, suppressing my impulses. I sensed around myself a sort of armor of insensibility that prevented my nerves from vibrating, in spite of all the sad details that my conductor gave me regarding my father's illness.

The first houses of Saint-Roch appeared in the darkness that had gradually fallen. Then the carriage stopped. We had arrived.

The little paternal shop had a lugubrious appearance, with its two counters encumbered by a chaos of porcelain and glassware, where here and there, as well as on the shelves, a smoky little lamp caused dull gleams to tremble. As I entered, my mother, who had heard the carriage, was already at the bottom of the narrow iron spiral staircase that linked the shop to the first floor. Her eyes were very red and resumed weeping at the sight of me; then she threw herself into my arms, a trifle theatrically, crying in a shrill voice:

"My poor . . . child."

My father had changed so much that I did not recognize him at all, with the result that it was impossible for me to lament as my mother was doing, who, standing at the foot of the bed with her handkerchief in her mouth, never ceased uttering a prolonged, continuous whine like the ululation of an osprey. The sensation of being among strangers dominated me again in a more imperious fashion and I gazed without a tear at that wan face, the skin taut over the cheekbones and upper jaw, which seemed to be laughing atrociously and painfully: a frightful face, lustrous with sweat, in which two white eyes were convulsed under excessively raised eyelids. I withdrew with a sensation of repulsion and fear.

My mother interrupted her ululation to say to me, in a broken voice: "Aren't you going to kiss your father, my child?"

I leaned over, understanding that I could not avoid that painful and futile duty, and, overcoming my disgust, I brushed the moribund's icy sweat hesitantly with my lips.

It was only long after my father had died that the chagrin of that death struck me. I can find no better comparison than the psychic phenomenon of what happens in the ears of certain preoccupied, pensive or distracted individuals who heed, hear and reply to a question a quarter of an hour after it has been asked. The impression must, therefore, remained suspended somewhere. That quarter of an hour, for me, was years, that's all. That slowness in perceptions and affective reactions is not, in any case, the working of a normal brain. I cannot help interpreting it, therefore, as a predisposition to *cerebral specialization*. That euphemism delights me, for the culmination of specialization is madness. Fortunate are the mediocre—anyone at all, "everybody"—who are perhaps cretins; they will never go mad.

Three years went by: three years of dogged study interrupted by bleak vacations alone with my desolate mother, who no longer had any concern except religious mummery and whose intelligence declined progressively under the weight of the chagrin caused to her by my father's death. Oh, I believe firmly that without Abbé Desmares, the only person in Saint-Roch with whom I could exchange a few ideas, I would have asked for the favor of spending my vacations at the college.

I had, moreover, become a model pupil, heaped with the best notes and compliments. My reports said: hard-working, intelligent, excellent mind. I arrived without shocks or any notable event at my baccalaureate, which I passed without the slightest difficulty, and then returned to Saint-Roch, which I quit definitively for Paris.

What did college take from me and what did it give me? Oh, that is quite evident. The experiment is within the range of everyone. The first time one touches a sensitive plant, it closes its leaves and folds its branches along its stem; the tenth time it only shudders slightly; the twenty-fifth time it is inert. I believe that I was that sensitive plant. Fundamentally, I had an affectionate nature, ready for expansion. I never found an opportunity or an example in my parents' home. By virtue of pride I have a sort of instructive mistrust, entirely guarded in relation to myself.

College hardened me; it stripped me of familial affection; it taught me egotism and isolation; it showed me that in life, it is "every man for himself and no one for all," it enabled me to see that it is by means of vices that one reigns and imposes oneself, and that sensibility is the blood of the soul, by means of which life trickles away drop by drop, until one dies of it.

If I had a son and wanted to raise him for myself, to love him and to make myself loved, I would never send him to a college; if I wanted to raise him for his own good, to construct in him a heartless atheistic brigand—everything it is necessary to be today in order to live in our modern world—I would intern him between the four walls of a boarding-school.

VI

PARIS!

Oh, I remember very well the afternoon when I arrived there, one frightfully bleak afternoon at the end of October. At the station I had a great deal of difficulty finding a cab because of the rain that was falling incessantly, with a monotonous little patter of small, dense droplets on the pointed paving-stones of the platform . . .

As I set foot on Parisian soil, in the midst of all those people hastening past, under the inquisitive eye of the customs officers, I experienced a poignant sensation of isolation . . . And, my valise in hand, my expression bleak and my manner pitiful, I gazed in a melancholy fashion at the brilliant streaks of the rain obliquely striping the high gray walls of the houses opposite.

I knew approximately where to go. When I left, Abbé Desmares, the deacon of Saint-Roch, had given me a letter of recommendation for the manager of a building whom he knew, at number 65 Rue de

Madame,[1] behind the Luxembourg. It was there that I had myself taken. The house had a tranquil appearance that seduced me from outside, but the staircase made me pull a face; it was dark and sweated a mixture of damp and dirt. The manager, however, Monsieur Sadran, a small man with little gray eyes always in movement, who appeared to me to be a former valet de chambre, welcomed me with all sorts of obsequious bows and mellifluous protestations.

"Monsieur will be very comfortable here," he stammered, rolling his little eyes. "If Monsieur seeks silence in order to work, he could not have fallen better. If Monsieur sometimes wishes to eat at home, the house's kitchen is excellent; furthermore, the greatest liberty . . ."

And he insinuated to me, in conclusion, that he had excellent wines for fine diners . . . Then he asked me for news of Abbé Desmares, who came to Paris four times a year, he told me, to spend a week . . . He was a liberal man, very respectable. What did he mean by "liberal" and "respectable," that little man?

He showed me ten rooms. I decided in favor of a large room on the fifth floor, very airy. I felt an irresistible need for light and space. It seemed to me that I would not have been able to live if I had been condemned, like so many others in Paris, to inhabit a little courtyard and only to participate in the rare oxygen that is so meanly rationed. My need for air and space

---

1 65 Rue Madame (which is rendered Rue de Madame on some stone inscriptions) is the site of a building now known as the Hôtel de l'Avenir.

is singular. It has always existed in me. I remember, when I was very small, having almost died of fright one day because, having set out to crawl under a small aqueduct ten meters long with an opening scarcely fifty centimeters wide, my lungs were suddenly strangled about half-way by the atrocious anguish of not being able to get out. I had an impression of being crushed between the stones; it seemed to me that I had a mountain on my breast and that I was about to choke. When I emerged I was sweating copiously and my arteries were beating at a gallop.

My first year in Paris offers nothing in particular. I worked from morning until evening in my room, if not with enthusiasm, at least with ardor. I never went out except to go to the hospital. I had arranged with Sadran for him to supply me with meals in my room at a very acceptable price—with the result that I was completely ignorant, not merely of Paris but even of the Latin Quarter.

One morning in February I had just returned from my hospital and I was waiting for the frugal breakfast that Sadran was to bring me when there were two raps on my door. I said "Come in," believing that it was my breakfast, although I had not recognized the hotelier's footfalls. My visitor, whom I considered with all the more astonishment because it seemed to me that I had "seen his face somewhere," took a step into my room and looked at me, smiling, without saying anything.

Although the face was not absolutely unfamiliar, the costume did not give me any information. The newcomer was wearing a neatly-tailored sea-blue jacket over the fantasy of a cream waistcoat embroidered with polychromatic florets. His trousers, with broad mauve checks, fell over varnished boots "in the latest fashion," his top hat had a shine that advertised an undeniable freshness.

As he continued to remain silent, allowing a mysterious smile to wander over his carefully shaven lips, I said: "To whom do I have the honor of speaking?"

My visitor uttered a burst of joyous laughter and exclaimed: "What! Don't you recognize me, Marie-Joseph?"

"Abbé Desmares!" I said, amazed.

It was, in fact, Abbé Desmares, but an Abbé Desmares rejuvenated and clean, absolutely unrecognizable in that costume. Abbé Desmares in civilian dress! Heaps of questions crowded my head.

My astonishment was so manifest that the abbé was obliged to remark upon it.

"Come on," he said, in a bantering tone, "are you shocked by something so trivial?"

"Trivial!" I stammered.

"Oh, my boy, if it's your first astonishment, be sure that it won't be your last. In any case, although I think you're still too young to give you a full explanation of my conduct, I hold you in high enough esteem and know you to be intelligent enough not to dissimulate with you. But let's pass over that for now and go have breakfast."

We went through the Luxembourg, entirely leafless, and then he headed, without searching, like a man who knows where he is going, for a restaurant in the vicinity of the Odéon. Alongside the ground floor hall there was a steep staircase above which was written: *Entrance to Salons and Cabinets, go up to the first floor.* We took it. At the top, a waiter hastened to relieve us of our hats and overcoats. And as he opened the door of a cabinet in which libertine prints were reflected in a large mirror furrowed with cracks, above a faded divan, dotted here and there with bizarre stains, the waiter murmured discreetly: "Bubbly, as usual?"

The abbé nodded his head, while scanning the menu, and as his back was turned to the mirror I remarked that his hair did not have at all the same cut as at Saint-Roch, and that his tonsure was so cleverly dissimulated that it seemed to be, at the most, a commencement of baldness . . .

These details are not superfluous. It is from that first visit of Abbé Desmares that what he called "my first astonishment" dates, which was, in truth, for me a veritable upheaval in ideas, which is to say—it is necessary that the first benchmark be planted—my first cerebral commotion. It is all the more notable—but not marked, alas, with a milestone—because I took a long time to recover.

The immediate effect was singular, to say the least. My piety had always been rather lukewarm, a lack of enthusiasm increased by my parents' fervor. "Like father, like son" is a simple absurdity. My father was an obese and ridiculous legitimist bigot. I am thin and pale; if I had been politically-inclined I would have been a communard; in any case, I am a revolutionary and the motive that determines the majority of my actions is not a vague and indeterminate vanity, like most people, but the very special vanity that is called fear of ridicule.

As for religion, I had just enough, on arriving in Paris, to go to take communion once a year, at Easter, as the Commandment requires, and go to mass on Sunday.

Well, on the Sunday following the departure of Abbé Desmares I did not go to mass. It seemed to me that I would see the officiating priest in a blue jacket and check trousers, and that the choirboy, at the consecration, would murmur discreetly to the officiant, while pouring the communion wine into the chalice: "Bubbly, as usual?"

That was a sort of hallucination, which haunted me painfully for nearly three years, every Sunday morning, until the day when I broke resolutely and definitively with all religious practice by abstaining from making my annual communion.

If I am so afraid of ridicule, it is because I have an exaggerated sentiment of it. Everyone is familiar with the grotesque head of Christ with black eyes who displays his olive complexion and beautiful curly beard in the shop windows of all the merchants of pious books and objects, with the label below that makes passers-by smile: "It is sufficient to look for an instant to see Christ open his eyes." An ingenious artist has imagined that divine plaything *ad usum delphini* [1] a

---

1 Literally, "for the use of the dauphin," used with reference to expurgated works—"Bowdlerized" in the English usage—Louis XIV having had special text prepared produced for the use of his eldest son.

lame hypocrisy; he has painted slightly blurred eyes on the lowered eyelids so that one can *ad libitum* see the eyes closed or open. It is sickening cretinism. The first time I saw it I could not forbid myself a foolish irritation, and I went into the shop seething, in order to cry to the merchant, to his profound stupefaction, my indignation and disgust at seeing the figure of Christ passed into the state of a "question of the day."

VIII

IT is evident that my faith was not very solidly founded, since it was, along with the civilian transformation of the deacon of Saint-Roch, the ridiculous image of that insipid "savior of humankind" that drove me away from the church. Furthermore, I confessed that ingenuously to Abbé Desmares during his second voyage in May, counting in advance ion the egotistical satisfaction of provoking his heartbroken protestations, for which I had prepared a bitter response: "All that is your fault!"

But the sly philosopher responded to me, with his eternal mocking laugh:

"I know, I know, my lad. A little science draws one away from God, a lot brings one back. You're still at the ABC of life and you permit yourself to judge! You haven't yet read within your soul; the *know thyself* of the ancients is still a dead letter for you, and you have the pretention to fathom loins and consciences! Get away—I've seen others . . ."

"But . . ." I attempted.

"Would you like me to tell you, once and for all, that God exists independently of religion, that religion exists independently of its ministers and that the latter aren't responsible for the selling of an image that is perhaps ridiculous, but in any case inoffensive?"

"Hold on," I said to him, suddenly. "Explain to me why you became a priest."

He looked me directly in the face, in the eyes, and took a pinch of snuff with a sonorous sniff.

"Is it necessary to speak frankly?"

"Of course. I'd finally like to learn something, and leave the a, b, c, d, for the grammar."

"I'll answer you, Marie-Joseph, although I'm convinced that it won't be to your advantage. The example of others, their advice and their experience, all of that, you see, is rubbish, as they say in Saint-Roch. One only learns what one learns at one's own expense. But what you want from me, above all, is glimpses of life rather than appreciations, isn't it?"

I nodded my head affirmatively.

"Why did I become a priest? Well, for the same reason as many others. I was the son of a peasant. On the farm, I had been brought up with the idea that the estate of curé was a good estate, in which one earned 'good money' and lived tranquilly, sheltered from all the troubles of life. That was the point of departure. At the seminary, when I began to reason on my own account, I said to myself that 'curés don't do military service . . .' Aha! You made a movement, I expected that . . ."

I stammered: "But what about the vocation?"

"Euphemism. Read: idleness. And, for me, the insurmountable horror of the brutality, the noise, the bragging, the ironware and the promiscuity with crapulous brutes—in sum, everything that militarism entails."

I was bewildered. I insinuated again: "But the Sacrifice of the Mass, the Eucharist!"

"Symbols, that's all."

"Then the hosts that bleed . . ."

"Many others are recounted. Jonah and the whale! Joshua stopping the sun! The world created in six days! Yes, I know, for the needs of the cause *days* have been transformed into *periods*, and it's said that the translators had misunderstood and that it was the rotation of the Earth that Joshua suspended . . . oh, stupidities, my boy, people say them every day . . . and you won't find many people to talk to you the way I'm doing."

My interlocutor could not suspect the immense disturbance into which that conversation threw me. He certainly did not think that I had spent those first six months of my student life in my room, in private with Sappey's anatomy,[1] and that, in consequence, I had remained the same as I was on leaving the college. The hospital had taught me a great deal, but it had not given me faith in medicine—far from it. I saw it groping every morning and recognizing its impotence every morning. The hospital had thrown

---

1 Marie-Philibert-Constant Sappey (1810-1896) published a significant *Traité d'anatomie descriptive* in 1847-63, an updated second edition of which was published in 1867-74; it became the standard textbook of French medical schools, much as "*Gray's Anatomy*" became the Bible of English medical education.

me abruptly face to face with human suffering, and I had observed that all their plaints did not afflict their faces with any rictus of revolt, but that one read there, on the contrary, the despondency of ruination; and I had concluded that this life is so made that it has all dolors as its share because all joys were in the other. In the other! That was what, moving from deduction to deduction, I now doubted, after desolate conversations that never ended, conversations of which I am only noting the general impression and from which I withdrew prey to a bleak dejection and an indefinable sadness.

One evening, I risked the question that had been burning my lips for a long time.

"What about Woman?"

Abbé Desmares started to laugh. "Ah, that's a question . . . a big question. Well, my lad, it's not a volume that's needed to resolve it, it's an entire library. Even the Bibliothèque National wouldn't be sufficient. So I'll only say two words to you. What is a woman? A safety-valve, and thus, not an end but a means. Society, as you'll see later, is divided into two classes: those who make woman a goal, and, what's more, *the* goal—and they are imbeciles—and those who reduce her to the state of a means; they're the wise."

The abbé took a strong dose of snuff and added, coldly:

"And I'm one of the latter . . ."

"You!"

"Ah, yes, the celibacy of priests! An invention of Gregory VII, definitively established by an edict of the Council of Trent. Well, the Church was able to say: 'You shall not marry,' making a sacrifice to the gallery, but it hasn't said: 'You shall not be a man.' The arteries, be sure of it, beat under a soutane as well as under a sea-blue jacket. In olden days they were more straightforward than today. For a long time we were left free to marry, and the Council of Nicea in 325 even rejected a motion ordering celibacy. I've explained to you and you've seen how, at Saint-Roch, I shield myself against temptation. I found the means of not allowing any skirt to come into my room. The perfume they emit enervates slumber and eroticizes dreams. Which doesn't prevent that, four times a year, when the seasons change . . ."

"But what becomes of the *cave mulierem* with which you prearmed my adolescence?"

"To begin with, I wanted above all to retard in you the blossoming of desire. By chance, you had remained improbably pure. I tried to enable you to continue thus, for reasons of health, for as long as possible. Then, I was afraid of your nature; I wanted to distance you from Woman because I feared that you might love her with your heart, with your ardent soul, with your seething brain and your generous ardor. That was the danger. If you had loved thus at twenty you'd be doomed. That's what my *cave mulierem* meant. It doesn't matter to me whether you . . . satisfy a need; that's natural, normal and obligatory; what's necessary is that your brain and your heart aren't preoccupied . . ."

I trembled convulsively with a frightful emotion, which my interlocutor did not seem to see. I was like Adam when he had just eaten the apple picked from the tree of good and evil; I suddenly saw clearly, and that clarity blinded me and I sensed that I was naked . . .

I stammered, again: "What of chastity, then?"

The abbé coughed his sarcastic laughter.

"Ha ha ha! Chastity! Hypocrisy or lure! No one is chaste. You hear me—no one! Physiological clowns have been seen striving for the *tour de force* of going for two months without eating—but only for two months. *Est modus in rebus.*[1] Nothing is absolute, not even, and above all, chastity. Take the word of an old confessor into whose sack many other sacks have emptied. You know the old precept, as old as the world and always as new, of your master Hippocrates: *Quotidie . . . Mense . . . Hebdomade . . .*[2]

"Yes. So what?"

"Well, it's a program for physiological health and, you know, for psychological equilibrium; it's necessary that the physiology be so: *mens sana in corpore sano.*

The bewilderment of those theories conducted me to a mute melancholy that the chief of service whom I continued to frequent assiduously at the Hôpital Laennec was obliged to diagnose, by the pinched

---

1 "There is a middle ground in things," quoted from Horace's *Satires*, the essence of such English phrases as "happy medium" and "golden mean," and the French political philosophy of the *juste milieu*.

2 "Once a day . . . a week . . . a month . . ."

81

aspect of my face, in the same way that he read the fatigue in my hollow eyes and on my ravaged features. I had already perceived for several mornings that he was looking at me askance during the round. Finally, one day, as we were going down to the consultation he said to me abruptly, quietly.

"What's the matter with you? Have you found a hair on your mistress's pillow that isn't yours?"

I replied rather hotly: "I don't have a mistress."

An extern who knew me slightly because he also lived in Père Sadran's house but respected my antisocial inclination without understanding it, intervened and said, crudely: "Daucy, a mistress! What would that virgin do with one?"

The chief had stopped abruptly.

"Get away! How old are you?"

"Twenty-one."

And you're . . . a rosebush! That explains everything—that complexion, those eyes, that bleak expression. But my friend, do you know where that leads, at your age? Well, it leads to hypochondria. And you know that hypochondria is the sheath of madness. Reflect, what I've just said to you is very serious. Draw conclusions from it . . . practical ones . . ."

IX

A S I grew older—and I grew older quickly, in months that were worth years—the more the stupidity and futility of life appeared to me. Why were people alive? Why was I alive? Some people have a goal: glory, ambition, the recompenses of the other life: virtualities, mirages, which exist because they believe in them. Others are drawn by the motive of doing what they imagine to be good: some want wealth, work a good part of their life to obtain it, and, when they have it, act as if they don't. I don't feel sorry for them; they still have the illusion of a goal. But how many others are miserable, not enjoying meager material joys in the present and not being able to console themselves with hope for the future. Those are the most numerous, for whom the flesh has misfortune and misery—for what are they living? They remind me of the placid and resigned squirrel who climbs untiringly the steps of his iron wheel. Does he think that it's an endless wheel? Do they think that it's an endless life?

I know masons in Saint-Roch who earn three francs a day for fifty years: just enough to shelter them from cold and hunger; their wives are laundresses and their work brings in thirty sous. They both return home exhausted by their day, collapsing with fatigue, mute and bleak, only having the strength to swallow the communal soup and not enough to enjoy the permitted caresses; they remain strangers to one another all their lives, and die almost without having known one another; they die without even having put ten francs aside for the illness that might arrive, and fortunately hasn't arrived.

Well, why do they go on living? Why do they drag that cannonball that weighs upon their foot and bruises their flesh? Why don't they cut the chain?

Ah, it's because their brain, from which, fortunately, no education has ever dispelled the fog, is never preoccupied with any problem; and it's because they have always seen their life heavy like that, from father to son, and from father to son their resigned shoulders have not shrugged off the burden, even though they have no faith in the future, because they remember the past. Hence their admiring and respectful consideration for the bourgeois, the fortunate of the earth, who only have to make the money their father made for them to bear fruit, and for whom repose is not the goal but only the occupation of existence.

How many individuals have never secreted a thought that is truly theirs? How many people are only a stomach and a belly? How many are there for whom living is merely fulfilling, for a certain lapse of time, a certain number of physiological functions, and whose unique preoccupation is going in quest of them anxiously every morning and supervising amorously the more-or-less reassuring fashion in which those important functions are accomplished. They don't suffer from life and they don't think of quitting it; on the contrary, they cling to it with all the strength of their organism, all the power of their terror of quitting their material joys; and they treat as sick those who escape from it, expelled by heartsickness.

Those reflections, and many others of analogous bitterness, came to me as a consequence of the strange counsel to visit prostitutes that my chief of service gave me with such a perfect serenity of soul. So debauchery, hideous debauchery, is general!

A man acts, and his flesh leads him. A man believes himself to be free but is kept on a leash by his passions; he is the plaything of his reflexes and, the eternal dupe of his vanity, he mistakes for a voluntary action what is only an execution commanded by a need. The will is the "executive power," the "deliberating power" is physiology. The executive power never acts except in consequence of a decision taken by the deliberating power. Oh, poor human microbe, brace yourself in your bacterial pride!

"No one is chaste," affirms a sage priest. "Beware of yourself, presumptuous individual who prides himself on continence, madness is lying in wait for you," pronounces the sagacious physician!

And I listened to the melancholy voice of Musset singing within me:

Woe betide the man who allows debauchery
To plant the first nail within his left breast.[1]

That evening, as I was going out, determined to dine in Paris in order to give a little flight to the black butterflies that were flapping their wings in my skull, Costelle, the extern who had signaled me to the attention of the chief that morning, came into my room. Under the pretext to borrowing my Béclard's *Physiologie*[2] he came primarily to find out whether his revelation to the chief had offended me.

"Not at all," I assured him. "Why would the observation of an exact fact annoy me?"

Then we chatted.

He admitted to me frankly that he had nursed strong prejudices for a long time against me because of my love of solitude, a solitude uniquely relieved by the visits of an old monsieur, which seemed barely adequate.

"Barely?" I observed, smiling.

"Come on, confess," he said, to explain the *barely*, "that you're frightfully religious."

"I don't even know whether I believe in God."

Costelle seemed bewildered.

"Oh, well, you can boast of fooling everyone, then. But let's see," he went on, "if it isn't holiness, why do

---

1 The oft-quoted lines are from Alfred de Musset's verse drama *La Coupe et les lèvres*, first published in the *Revue de Paris* in 1831.

2 Jules-Auguste Béclard's standard textbook of physiology was first published in 1856.

you flee the society of men so much, and especially that of women?"

"You don't understand," I said. "I don't flee it; I don't seek it, that's all—do you see the difference?"

"There are moments, however, when a man is obliged at least to seek the society of a woman."

"I haven't yet experienced that . . . sentiment."

"Oh, you're delightful!"

After a few seconds of silence he went on: "Well, astonishing philosopher, since we're chatting, come and dine with me downstairs."

"Thank you, my dear friend, but the communal table horrifies me. On the other hand, I'd be very happy if you'd accept to dine at a little restaurant I know, where we'll eat well."

And I took him to Abbé Desmares' cabaret.

"Do you like white wine?" I asked him.

"Certainly."

"Well, waiter, give us some bubbly."

The dinner was very cheerful. Costelle ate well and drank copiously. His witty sallies were ironic and paradoxical in appearance because he never pronounced the expected phrase formulating the verity accepted by the general run of repeaters of current ideas. He was something of a southerner—not too much, just enough to give him verve. He launched ideas like rockets, noisily, and reveled in the deployment of their luminous and polychromatic display. He seemed absolutely infatuated with them, sustaining them flamboyantly and convinced that no one could possibly think the contrary. And when I insinuated, timidly: "Do you believe that?" Costelle stopped short and said:

"Eh? You don't think so? Perhaps so. After all, I don't hold to it excessively."

And he laughed, brightly and infectiously, uncovering his healthy white teeth.

When the bill was settled I suddenly said: "Costelle, my friend, I'm abominably drunk."

"Happily," he said, "you're not the only one."

In fact, I felt a mild drunkenness that slowly submerged my brain. Between me and the exterior there was something like the interposition of a glaucous but limpid liquid that entered into my ears, buzzing, and my eyes, the lids of which were fluttering. Objects appeared to me to be considerably enlarged, and sounds diminished. My friend spoke to me in a soft, slow, seemingly distant voice; it seemed to me that I had cotton wool in my ears that was filtering the sounds. And I felt very joyful, without cause, amused by everything and nothing, very good, my heart open, with an insatiable need for expansion, to love someone, to hold a woman in my arms and parade my lips over all her skin.

In the street we marched very straight, arm in arm, comfortably silent, hats slightly tilted back, with gleams of gaiety in our slightly troubled eyes and blissful smiles on our lips. Night had fallen, a clear, warm June night zigzagged by a flock of soft sounds, the causes of which it was impossible for me to determine precisely. We suddenly emerged into an immense avenue planted with superb trees, whose incomparably bushy foliage was entangled, as in a centenarian forest.

Vast sidewalks full of people bordered the causeway, so broad that the people opposite, on the terrace of a café, seemed very small.

"Where are we, then?" I exclaimed. "What is this magnificent boulevard?"

Costelle seemed as bewildered as me. "In truth," he said, "I have absolutely no idea. I'm seeing it for the first time. How the devil did we get here?"

"Let's try to read the plaque," I said.

We approached; the white letters danced before our eyes on their blue background. Gradually, however, the saraband stopped and we deciphered: "Boulevard Saint-Michel," seized by mad laughter that did not stop.

"Are we drunk enough?" exclaimed Costelle, joyously.

We kept walking, gripped by a need to burn off the stored alcohol by means of exercise. Suddenly, we stopped in front of a porch aureoled by light.

"Follow me," said Costelle.

"Where are you taking me?"

"Come on."

"What is this Alhambra?"

"Bullier, of course."[1]

Bullier! I did not see anything at first except vague rotations in a dust of light. I heard frenetic hurrahs, applause and clamors that left my ears buzzing for a few seconds. Then, in the black crowd, where women

---

1 At the time when the present story was published the famous music-hall known as the Bal Bullier was located in the Avenue de l'Obervatoire.

were making bright patches undulate in currents here and there, voids were suddenly hollowed out, into which I plunged, eyes wide, trying to see, infiltrating myself into hedges, insinuating myself between shoulders, emboldened by the "bubbly."

By virtue of the hazards of jostling I found myself abruptly shoved into the front rank of a thick hedge surrounding a quadrille. At first I saw nothing extraordinary legitimating that accumulation of the curious, the cries and acclamations. The two couples were turning correctly on the spot, holding one another by the hand. Then the rotations stopped, and in the circle vociferations resounded: "Chahut! Chahut!"[1] The female dancer who was facing me, on the other side of the quadrille, advanced alone, machine-gunned by two hundred gazes. She was a tall blonde with golden hair, quite pretty, her face as impassive as that of an Englishwoman, her dress very tight at the waist and bouffant over the breasts. She advanced while beating a succession of precipitate little entrechats, her head leaning alternately to the right and the left, with undulations of the hips and torso. She was holding her dress modestly between the thumb and index-finger, discreetly raised over a white underskirt bordered by a broad band of lace. She was so blonde, so graceful and so chaste that she gave the impression of designing an old-fashioned minuet.

1 *Le Chahut* [Uproar] was the slang term for a kind of high-kicking music-hall dance better known in England as the can-can. Georges Seurat's famous painting with that title was exhibited at the Salon des Indépendants in 1890, where Trézenik surely saw it.

And the cries redoubled: "Chahut! Chahut! Higher!"

Then the pretty blonde lifted her skirt, which she shook in order to make the others slide, her rings sparkled, and in a seething of white things her ankles appeared, slim and tapering, clad in stockings circled by thin multicolored strips, and her plump feet, in tight, very open shoes braced on high heels. Then she curbed herself in a savant gesture that showed off the white omega of her breasts through the gaping dress, and, suddenly straightening up, she disappeared all the way to the eyes behind a cloud of floating lace and whirling skirts, which simulated a colossal white rose in which all the festoons of underskirts were grouped like a tremulous corolla, and from which emerged, like a charming symbolic pistil, admirable legs gartered by a cascade of mauve ribbons: the legs of a modern Venus, of a pure design and a model pleasing to the eye, simultaneously muscular and lithe, issuing from the batiste of bloomers so tenuous and diaphanous that one might have thought them pink.

An admiring rumor rumbled in the circle of spectators.

Now very close to me, she leapt up momentarily on one foot, the other in the air, and fell back abruptly in a swirl of skirts, which slapped me in the face with their wind, impregnated with iris and aroma of woman. Then there was an immense clamor, and I glimpsed the dancer, in a flash, being carried away in triumph, perched on the shoulders of a howling group, toward the garden . . .

It was only then that I perceived that I had lost Costelle in the crowd.

X

"HEY, Daucy!"

How many hours had I been turning, letting myself go with the flow, thought lost, gazing internally at that leg in the air, which I could still see, with its cambered calf, its fine stocking, its garter easy on the eye and the little band of snow that the short bloomers had allowed to be seen as they slid. What, that was it, hideous debauchery? Ha ha! Hideous! That pleases you to say, Morality of my Fathers! But does your "hideous" not resemble the "I'm not hungry" of the sated diner?

And phrases droned in my head, colliding noisily: "No one is chaste . . ." "Woe betide the man who unleashes debauchery . . ." "Beware incontinence . . . !" "Hypochondria . . . !" Then, suddenly, in an abrupt return to the past, I heard the shrill voice of my mother yapping, crying to me every night when I extinguished my light: "Marie-Joseph, have you offered your heart to the good God?" And I murmured, my teeth clenched, turning toward that crowd where the crudest remarks were being brayed: "My heart to the good God! Oh, yes, the old jokes!"

A strange warmth invaded me . . . And still that leg . . . ! I could have counted the stripes on the stocking . . .

"Hey, Daucy!"

It was Costelle, who snatched me from my reverie. He was installed in front of a beer in the wooden gallery overlooking the hall. As I arrived next to him he squeezed the hand of a woman whom I recognized by virtue of having noticed her in a quadrille because of the singularly lascivious fashion in which she was dancing. She was a brunette, with night-black hair. The irises of her eyes were so dark that they were confounded with the pupils, which gave her a strange gaze of an extreme vivacity and acuity, shining like the eyes of a wild beast in the midst of her mat complexion, the expression of which it was impossible to define. She had lips so red that one might have thought that they were bleeding, and her lower jaw advanced beneath the upper in an animal fashion that compelled attention. When she spoke, something like a laugh trembled in the depths of her voice, so that she seemed simultaneously to be mocking herself, what she said and the person to whom she was saying it.

I considered her for a long time, and she appeared to remark and to encourage my attention. She was clad in a loosely-fitting dress that did not make any line of her body precise or emphasize any relief, permitting imaginations to wander at their ease, but the breadth of her shoulders and the slenderness of her waist, which it was impossible to hide, revealed that she could not be unshapely. Unlike the majority of women, who took the temperature as a pretext for exhibiting as much of their bosom as they could, Antonia—I learned her name subsequently—had a high neckline and her tight sleeves descended all the way to her thin wrists, which no jewelry adorned. Dancing was not a pretext for showing the color of her stockings and unveiling the perfume of her undergarments; she danced with her hips like a bayadere, and the mime of her face stimulated a tempest of tumultuous frissons in your skin.

She addressed me abruptly when she saw me sit down beside Costelle.

"Well, Monsieur, will you be more amiable than your friend? I'm thirsty, and this oaf won't buy me a beer."

I understood that Costelle's refusal was prompted by his apprehension of annoying me. I blushed violently and stammered: "Will you permit me to offer you one, Madame?"

"I believe I would permit it! Hey Louis, a tub!"

She sat down between us, smiling. Her smile was singular. It resembled the rictus of a pretty animal that is about to bite. It only uncovered the upper jaw, a pink jaw planted with little very white teeth, as narrow and pointed as the teeth of a saw. I could not think of anything to say to her, all the more so because a heady perfume exhaled from her that reawakened my drowsy intoxication and whipped my blood. I could not find anything but a stupid question:

"How good you smell. What gives you that scent?"

She responded with a laugh that resembled the trill of a trumpet.

"It's my natural perfume, Monsieur!"

Then, after having stared at me for a second with her disquieting gazeless eyes, she sniggered.

"Well, Thomas, come and see if you don't believe it!"

Abruptly, she had taken my head under her arm and plastered my face against her armpit . . .

I got up from there so pale, with eyes so flamboyant that Costelle was alarmed and murmured: "Be careful, Antonia, he's drunk . . ."

The prostitute stared at me, amazed by my disturbance.

"Damn," she said placidly, "it doesn't take much to light you up!"

I had risen to my feet, my arteries on fire, my temples beating the charge, and my brain boiling; I had just been bitten by the sharp tooth of desire; I felt myself gripped, invaded entirely, impelled by an incoercible need to possess that woman *immediately*. I felt that I no longer belonged to myself and that a resistance on her part might drive me to irreparable woes. I was no longer pale; my blood was circulating with an unusual violence, and I felt my ears buzzing, where the vehemence of the pulse-beats deafened me and injected my eyes with blood, blinding me to such a point that I was obliged to sit down. I had something akin to a forge in my skull, where hammers were pounding in cadence . . .

I swallowed three large glasses of sugared water in succession and recovered my senses somewhat.

Antonia stared at me curiously, as one stares at a phenomenon, and said, with slight mockery: "It's true that you still have it?"

I got up, quite lucid now but absolutely obsessed by my desire. I replied: "Would you like us to go to your place?"

"Just like that! Right away!" she joked. "That's nice . . . !"

I was shaken by a frisson that made me tremble from head to foot. My contracted jaws could scarcely articulate a word. I nodded my head.

It is probable that Costelle had convinced her in advance, for she passed her arm under mine with the best grace in the world, while the student traced a weary benediction in the air and disappeared into the crowd.

"Why are you trembling like that?" Antonia said, as we traversed the causeway toward the cab-stand. But almost immediately, dispensing me from responding to her observation, she added: "On, but it's not worth the trouble of taking a cab; I live close by."

"Where do you live, then?" I asked, glad of an apposite subject of conversation.

"Rue Saint-Jacques, almost at the corner of the first street on the right. But before then, *cheri*, you'll pay for a supper—just here, at the Grenouille—I'm hungry."

I shook my head and dragged her, rather churlishly, toward her dwelling.

"My God, you're in a hurry," she said, resignedly. "Come on, a little sooner, a little later . . ."

I fell back into a bizarre, feverish, preoccupied silence full of heat that rose in waves, casting blood into my eyes, clawed by an imperious desire that I felt impotent to muzzle, which was bellowing with rage, and captivated all my attention to such a point and took possession so completely of my thought, that I could no longer find a word to say, in spite of the efforts I made to extract myself from that obsession . . .

We were engulfed in a corridor so narrow that my two elbows brushed it, and so completely devoid of light that the prostitute was obliged to give me her hand in the darkness in order to guide me up the steps of a steep staircase where I stumbled at almost every step. On the second floor she stopped, took a latch-key from her pocket, and then a box of candle-matches. The taper illuminated a kind of narrow reception room papered in vivid red. To the right and the left, two doors were dissimulated by thick red curtains. She opened the one on the left, introduced me into a room where she lit two candles and said: "Get undressed; I'll be back."

And she disappeared. It seemed to me that she opened the other door and that a sort of gasp emerged during the second that she took to open and close the door.

Drunkenness had gripped me again. Objects were spinning around me and it was as if I had a dolorously oppressive weight on my lungs. I glimpsed, vaguely, a high bed on which the eiderdown bulged like a belly, under red curtains festooned with white guipure. The rest was confused, in the whirl, in a red circle, patched here and there with white, which enclosed me hermetically. I had the hallucinatory sensation of being imprisoned in a ball without an opening. I was, however, sitting on the floor, more or less undressed, and, after painful efforts, slid between the sheets, impregnated with a strong perfume that gave a whiplash to my intoxication.

From time to time I had a metallic crescent around my forehead, the two extremities of which tightened, compressing my temples violently; it seemed to me that under that pressure, my head was flattened and my forehead bulged, like that of a hydrocephalus. Then a movement was produced in the bed, a gently rocking movement that lulled me, occasionally interrupted by a sudden violent pitching that sometimes approached my head to the ceiling and sometimes my feet.

I tried to get up, but the muscles of my limbs were as if paralyzed and would not move. And the rocking took hold of me again; I rocked and rocked . . . The candle, veiled by gray lampshades, bathed the room with a watery light, troubled and shifting . . .

I fell asleep . . .

XI

I was woken up by cries in the street.

"Green peas! Green peas! Potatoes by the bushel! Potatoes!"

Pale daylight was coming from the window in spite of the closed Venetian blinds and the heavy curtains. In the penumbra of the room I perceived my garments, scattered on the floor or draped on chairs, pell-mell with Antonia's skirts and stockings. She was asleep, her face to the wall. I could hear her tranquil breath, hissing between her open lips.

Suddenly, a discreet finger tapped on the door. Antonia turned over and propped herself up on her elbow. I did not move and closed my eyes again. I sensed her holding her breath in order to listen better, and rubbing her eyes in order to expel the torpor of sleep. Someone knocked again, two slightly clearer raps. And Antonia murmured, taking care not to wake me: "Come in."

And I heard the friction of the opening door on the carpet. A dry voice said:

"I believe that it's time."

Antonia stepped over me gently, without replying, and I heard the rustle of the skirt that she put on precipitately.

What's all this? I thought, sickened by my night, my mouth and my mind thick with disgust.

Antonia went out, and I could not resist any longer my haste to flee. My skin was painful, overrun by itching. An irresistible desire clawed me to plunge myself as quickly as possible into a purifying bath, in which all the shame would dissolve of that bestial night, and I could cleanse myself of those kisses and caresses, those embraces and enlacements in the folly of which I had sought pleasure and had only found a nauseating scorn for human beings abusing themselves with such turpitudes.

I wanted to slip away silently, after having left in plain sight on the marble of the mantelpiece the regulation offering. But the doorknob that I turned very gently suddenly grated, and as I arrived in the little reception room I saw the other door open and Antonia appeared, closing the batten very quickly behind her—but not so quickly that I did not see, in the rapid gap, two large candles like church candles burning on the nightstand, illuminating the profile of a woman lying motionless on her back in the bed with a crucifix in her joined hands. Her face was so pale and her features so drawn that it could only be a cadaver.

The prostitute understood by my attitude what I had seen. She thought it obligatory to give me a few words of explanation. It was a comrade, ill for a long time, who had just died. Oh, life was not fundamentally what it appeared to be on the surface. She had had a hard time recently; it was necessary to work for two. The physician didn't bestir himself for nothing. Once, there had been one who took payment in kind, but he hadn't come back. And then, those thieving pharmacists didn't give their drugs away!

She interrupted herself to express her astonishment at seeing me dressed so quickly. I stammered some vague explanation: medical student . . . the hospital . . . rounds . . .

Antonia did not insist. She simpered. "You're content with me? You'll come back?" Then, leaping abruptly from one subject to another, she said, laughing, in a low voice because of the dead woman: "Well, you know, you didn't have your cockade yesterday evening . . . I'll wager that you don't know what you did to me . . ."

I stammered, in a hurry to avoid her revelations: "No, but adieu, adieu, I'm already late."

"Well, *cheri*," Antonia said, as I gave her a last handshake on the landing, "it would be kind of you, if it wouldn't disturb you greatly, to put this letter in the post."

In the street, I looked at the address. It was written in a hesitant and seemingly hasty hand, and I noticed that it was scarcely sealed; the gum, licked by a hasty tongue, had not adhered everywhere. Almost immediately, I was tormented by a violent and feverish desire to violate that careless seal and to read the letter that hazard had placed in my hand, and which, I was sure, would uncover a corner of the mystery of life . . .

I turned it over and over, irritably, my impatient fingers crumpling it nervously, and suddenly, moved by an impulsion that my momentarily-paralyzed will was impotent to master, my index finger slipped abruptly into the gap in the envelope, the flap of which, as if it were conniving with my culpable and morbid curiosity, was detached with a little dry click.

The ardor of my desire to read that letter was so strong that it was only on reflection, a long time after, that the infamy of my action became apparent to me; but at the time, the dull growl of my conscience was stifled and I only heard an *order*, come from I know not where—certainly not from my reason, my will or my intelligence—so imperious that I could not disobey, to read that letter.

I note that detail especially because it was the first impulsive action in which I was obeying without argument, because it was the first time that my will, always sovereign and dominant, was beaten in the breach. The next day, it is true, having recovered my senses, I found the explanation that the event occurred after a night of nervous excitement that had evidently lessened my will-power. Physical exhaustion and mental exhaustion held sway and were in command. I was weak physically and weak morally. That is quite natural.

It is quite natural, but was that excuse for my fault, an explanation of the first symptom, not a new cowardice, an ingenious but wretched artifice, trying, perhaps unconsciously, to deceive my sagacity?

This is the letter. I copied it and conserved it as a cynical and sickening document before putting it in the post. It was addressed to Monsieur X. X***, man of letters, rue ***, Paris: the name of a failure devoid of talent but full of bile and envy, who had never been able to have anything printed in a daily newspaper and who died of jaundice. I have not changed a comma.

My dear friend,

*I told you in my last letter that I would soon have recovered entirely; I'm sorry to tell you the contrary. A few days after my first letter I fell back into my state of weakness. My friend had the doctor come, who gave her to understand that it would take an enormous time and exceptional care to render me to health; he says that I am very weak, worn out, and feared from one day to the next a serious peritonitis. For myself, my poor X***, I'm finished, on the way out; either I'm much mistaken, or this will be my last letter.*

How glad I am to be going, for I sense and confess with terror that I have become wretched.

Poor friend, if, as I suppose, you have remarked my decline, feel sorry for me, don't scorn me, for I've endured every-thing—hunger, tortures and sarcasms— always conserving deep down a feeble hope of recovery.

Today, all is lost, for I no longer have any courage, passions or health—in a word, nothing of what can aid a woman to emerge from the mud.

I no longer have anything but hatred, a desire for vengeance against all men, handsome or ugly, young or old, whose villainy I know, and who, not content with making me slake their filthy passions, play with my hunger, lifting the siege without paying or, wanting to profit from my vice, pushed audacity further, to the point of scorning me and insulting me.

My friend, I am dying of the chagrin of having become so base, so vile; for it is necessary to say everything: while I was living with you, weary of running around agencies and shops, in vain, I whored, and it's that which has doomed me—so utterly that I desire wholeheartedly to finish with life rather than fall even further.

It is more than probable that when you read this letter I shall be six feet underground; in any case, I am going to give you my address so that you can obtain news of me. I forgive you for your petty perversities, which had the goal of pushing me to work, and I hope that you will forgive me, similarly, for the involuntary harm that I have done you.

If I have any advice to give you, it is to renounce your ideas of glory and fortune; that dream without realization might kill you, as it has killed my dream of rehabilitation.

Darling, have courage, and, above all, work; do not attach yourself to anyone; affection and amour are only follies.

Adieu, on earth, and au revoir *in a happier world.*

Your only friend,
Louise

One final word.

I have reflected for a long time on the scant underwear that I have and I thought that, by placing it with the laundress that you know I could, in case I live, retrieve it, or, in case of death, that you can retrieve it and use it to repair your own or make yourself linen in case of illness.

This is the list: three pairs of cotton stockings; one woman's chemise; four straight false collars; two white handker-chiefs; one handkerchief marked L with violet borders; two pair of white bloomers.

So that is it! The good life . . . *living the good life*, as they say, the good folk, with a *moue* of indignation upon their lips. The good life! That! Load of cretins!

XII

I have just reread the preceding pages, and it is with an undissimulated satisfaction that I do not observe any trace of incoherence there. The account is, on the contrary, precise, cold and methodical, and does not indicate any essential cerebral disturbance. Nevertheless, the final pages bear the marks of a keener interest in the subject-matter. The story of my life captivates me and I am recounting it with complaisance; I am not omitting any detail, and setting the scene in a puerile fashion. Why?

Why? Unconsciously, it is to prove to myself that my brain is still vibrant, that if my reason is tottering, it has not yet stumbled.

Then too, I have established this consoling observation: that my malady seems less radical since I have had the courage to look it in the face.

I have thus established that I am suffering from the expectation of a misfortune rather than the fact of that misfortune; from the apprehension rather than the reality.

Yes, to begin with, that is what I said to myself. Then, feeling that I was strong enough to attempt the decisive experiment, I went to Saint-Anne to compare the mental state of the internees to mine. And I came back from there with this terrible statement of Doctor Ball's in my notebook, heard in his lecture on the premonitory symptoms of general paralysis:[1]

"I have in my library volumes of verse whose inspiration is due to the intellectual stimulation of general paralysis. I know journalists in the French press, admired polemicists whose talent is admitted by anyone without contest but who owe all the verve and wit of their articles uniquely to the excitatory period of general paralysis."

Thus, the lucidity of the commencement, which reassured me, proves nothing. It might be due to "the excitatory period of general paralysis."

---

1 Benjamin Ball (1833-1893) was the first appointee to the chair of mental illness at Saint-Anne in 1877. His works included *De la morphinomanie* (1885) and *La Folie érotique* (1888). "General paralysis of the insane" was the contemporary term for mental aberrations associated with tertiary syphilis—a diagnosis that Ball played a part in popularizing, and which was said to account for about one in four of the internees of Saint-Anne and other Parisian mental hospitals in the *fin-de-siècle*. Numerous famous French writers of the period suffered from syphilis, and anyone with such a diagnosis would have been well aware of the potential dangers of that final phase. The cause of Léo Trézenik's death at the age of 47 is unrecorded, but Guy de Maupassant (1850-1893), whose novelette "Le Horla" (1887) is one of the classics of the subgenre to which *La Confession d'un fou* belongs, was driven mad by tertiary syphilis and tried to commit suicide in 1892 by cutting his own throat.

Oh, why did I go out there, to bring back, with that cruel statement, the poignant and dolorous impression that haunted me like a nightmare throughout my visit.

One morning, Costelle said to me: "Will you come to Saint-Anne on Sunday? Ball is lecturing on general paralysis, you know—the malady of men of letters, overwork, etc. It's interesting."

I went.

The entrance to Saint-Anne is almost cheerful. A long avenue of bushy chestnut trees bordered with flower-gardens takes you to the pavilions. We pushed, to the left, a large glazed door and penetrated into a sort of little park, grassy and shady, where men dressed in gray and coiffed with yokos were walking, some solitary and bleak, others in groups, sprightly and chatting. I thought I was in the garden of a hospital, in the presence of convalescents returning to health. Perhaps there were not only madmen at Saint-Anne.

I said to Costelle: "Who are all these patients?"

Costelle stared at me in astonishment. "But they're the madmen," he said.

I made a sort of backward movement. "What! The madmen!"

"Oh, yes—you thought they were all locked up. Oh, have no fear, the agitated are in cells; these are calm."

A patient approached us discreetly, his straw hat in his hand.

"Excuse me for disturbing you, Messieurs, but Monsieur"—he was addressing Costelle—"have you been thinking about me? Have you spoken to Monsieur Ball about me? Oh, Monsieur, I'm so unhappy to be here. I'm not mad, Monsieur, I'm not mad and only ask to prove it. If Monsieur Ball will give me the instruments I requested, you'll see, Monsieur, that I'm not mad . . ."

The poor fellow had a sad and benevolent expression that impressed me greatly. Nothing could be read in his mild expression but a dejected resignation, and there was no glimmer of madness there.

"Don't worry, my friend, and be reasonable," Costelle replied, "I'm occupied with you."

When he had drawn away, I could not help saying sharply to my friend: "Come on! That man isn't mad. Why is he interned?"

"He's a maniac," said Costelle placidly. "He's invented perpetual motion. This is his system, in brief: a water-wheel, with a waterfall that activates it and a basin underneath to collect the water; and, to perpetuate the motion—this is the snag—a siphon that takes the water from the basin and conducts it to the waterfall. No one can make him understand that the water will never rise up in his siphon, and, in consequence, that the wheel will stop when the waterfall runs out of water."

"I concede that it's . . . insensate, but in sum, he isn't dangerous, that inventor, so why intern him?"

"Because, at a given moment, he's susceptible to becoming furious, and killing."

"What! The fellow has such a placid appearance!"

"Suppose an argument in which he develops his theory; he's told brutally that he's an idiot, and becomes irritated; his interlocutor insists, he's exasperated, and is then prey to a fit of furious dementia. If he has a weapon to hand, he might commit a crime. Thus, society has the right to put him out of a state to do harm."

I was distressed, because a frightful thought had suddenly occurred to me: perhaps I am sicker than that man, capable of a murderous impulse; perhaps, if someone could read my mind, I'd be locked up.

What saves me, at least for the moment, is that I am conscious of my condition, that I can struggle against my impulses on the one hand, and, on the other, avoid until my last glimmer of reason, and the ultimate contraction of my energy, giving society weapons against me. But, will I always—or even for much longer—be able to struggle? Is not the hour imminent when dementia might put a weapon in my hand? Am I, too, so placid and so voluntary, not susceptible to becoming furious and killing?

That is where I am at present in my . . . illness. This return to myself, by means of this intimate journal, this look into the past, this voyage through heredity, has been, in sum, more helpful than I had any right to suppose. There is nothing terrible to fear from atavism. Perhaps, then, there is hope? But in the end, whence and how has this anguish come to me of which I am dying, this fear—perhaps justified—of going mad?

Whence?

Oh, I believe that I shall never forget that afternoon in May when the frightful idea that I might die insane crossed my mind for the first time.

It was in the Rue de Madame in summer; a heavy heat entered through the open window. I was reading a book of abstract philosophy on which all the active force of my brain was concentrated. A barrel-organ was playing, scarcely audible, in the distance. Imprecise sounds were rising from the street, buzzing through all the open windows. I had just raised my eyes to follow in flight an idea that my reading had caused to surge forth. Three o'clock chimed; I remember that detail.

Suddenly, it seemed to me that I no longer recognized my room. The sunlight, filtered with difficulty by the blind, illuminated it violently, and the hue and form of the furniture, the tint of the paper, the aspect of all my familiar objects and the general air of the room all appeared to me to have changed—and me too. An inexplicable phenomenon of duplication was operating within me. I saw myself gazing, I felt myself becoming astonished, and a terror rose within me, crazy and unanalyzable, without an object, a terror that made my skin prickle and caused large droplets of sweat to form there.

I stood up precipitately in order to chase away the strange obsession, but it persisted. I went to the mirror; I did not recognize myself. My ears were buzzing, my head seemed heavy, it seemed to be agitated by a kind of tremor and was swaying from right to left. I paced back and forth with long strides, and my footsteps resonated singularly. The floorboards had never had that sound. I made a movement to swallow my saliva—a painful movement, because my throat was dry, and I said aloud, determined to master even so the emotion that was taking hold of me: "Come on! This is stupid!"

But that attempt only augmented my terror. My voice had a strange timbre, as if veiled: the voice that one has in dreams. And suddenly, I started to laugh. The idea came to me that all this was only a nightmare. It frequently happens to me that I dream that I am dreaming.

That was it, of course; I was dreaming. But . . .

Someone suddenly knocked on my door, I shouted: "Come in!" But was that really me? It was definitely not my voice, the one that I usually had.

Costelle came in.

"Are you coming to dinner?" he said. Then he looked at me. "What's the matter with you? You're as pale as a figurant in the Morgue."

He told me subsequently that my eyes had the fixed gaze and the dilated pupils of the hypnotized. As my strange manner had already struck him in recent days he advanced toward me abruptly, put his hands on my shoulders and slapped me violently in the face.

"Why, what's got into you, old man," the medical student said. "Have you been doing experiments in autohypnosis? It's just that you've had such a bizarre air for some time."

I did not reply, because my eyes had just fallen on the dial of the clock.

"It's six o'clock," I murmured.

"Well, yes, it's six o'clock. Where the devil are you coming back from?"

"Where am I coming from? I don't know where I'm coming back from."

Thus, I remembered very well having heard three o'clock chime at the commencement of my . . . fit. I had remained in that state for *three hours*. There had been a sort of pause in my psychological life for three hours. For three hours my Self had escaped my direction, as well as my consciousness . . .

PART TWO

I

Ihave left this journal aside for six months, so great
was my disgust with everything, and my idleness in
formulating it was suddenly accentuated. And yet I
have come back to it, just as a coquette who feels herself
getting old returns to her mirror with the apprehension
of finding another wrinkle. For me, it is with the fear of
observing the progress toward the . . . malady.

Already, I no longer dare write the veritable word.
Six months.

I have quit the Rue Madame. The proximity of
Costelle had become insupportable to me. I could
no longer miss the hospital without that troublesome
chatterbox coming to relaunch me and demand
the reason for it. Then too, I no longer want to see
Abbé Desmares. That placid philosopher is odious
to me. He doesn't sense the harm he has done me,
that his deceptive conversations have done me. I have
disappeared.

I live in a fifth-floor room with a balcony in the
Place Daumesnil,[1] a few paces from the fortifications,

---

1 The Place Daumesnil is now called the Place Félix-Éboué; it

whose restful view extends from the butte of Père-Lachaise to the green masses of the Bois de Vincennes, No one will come to disturb my solitude. I have the esteem of my concierge because I never come back after ten o'clock, never get her out of bed and she has never found a skirt while doing my housework. And without fearing the indiscreet investigation of Costelle or the annoying arrival of the abbé, I can continue the ferocious and dogged analysis of my cracked Self, threatened with ruination.

This morning I received a letter from my mother. She complains bitterly that my studies are not advancing. I dare not tell her yet that I shall never be a "doctor"—that is the last terrestrial concern of the poor woman, who, Abbé Desmares told me during his last visit, no longer sees anything else but God. I dare not tell her that medicine disgusts me, that I have found commerce there where I sought science, and that I shall never be anything at all, because nothing exists . . .

That letter recalled me a little to reality, which I have an increasingly irresistible tendency to confound with a dream. For a few days, that has even been the cause of a rather intense mental suffering. I commenced by having absences—I can find no other word to characterize my state—very singular absences that I initially attributed to distraction, when my thought floats, indecisively, without settling on any subject whatsoever. I do not think. I cannot think.

surrounds the fountain of the Château d'eau, also known as the Fontaine aux lions.

Ideas have no clarity; it is as if they are sketched, and I scarcely glimpse them before their silhouette is already effaced; there is no better comparison than a design rapidly made on water, which disappears before the eye has been able to seize the outline. On those days it requires a superhuman effort of will to arrest my thought on a subject, however simple, and it is absolutely forbidden for me to delve into it and to extract deductions from it. And that causes me such suffering that a sweat rises on my face. On some evenings, I can scarcely read; I have lost the meaning of the words. It is necessary for me to read a phrase three or four times in order to understand.

I am subject to the effects of overwork without having the cause.

As well as those intellectual troubles, which I can still attribute to the congestive pressures of spring, I noted an excessive exaggeration of my habitual impressionability. Neurosis has made giant strides within me in six months.

I noted my first intellectual troubles above. My first moral troubles go back a long way. I have always had a penchant for lying. That aspect of my character did not worry me at first because I had observed that almost all children are boastful liars, that they all exaggerate everything connected with their parents; but that tendency, which is ordinarily reduced with age, was augmented in me to such an extent that as a young man I was always obliged to observe myself when I recounted to a third party some event that I had witnessed or in which I had participated as an actor. As a mere witness, I always embroidered, amplified and magnified, in order to appear to have seen something extraordinary; as an actor, I modified the role I had played, attributing words to myself that had only come to me on reflection and actions that I had ruminated subsequently, telling myself that I ought to have said this and ought to have done that. A little later I invented stories wholesale of accidents involving trams that I had witnessed and accounts of various complicated events that brought out my spirit of observation. When the story was told, disgust seized me for my stupidity and a revolt against the mediocrity of those satisfactions of self-esteem, and I made resolutions to control myself that I could not keep. Yes, I *could not*, for in those cases, the singular phenomenon from which I suffered many a time since, the mortal anguish, was reproduced in such a fashion that while *the liar* was placidly telling his story in great detail, *the other* shrugged his shoulders and grumbled, without being able to stop him: "Imbecile! Imbecile!"

The curious aspect of that bizarre movement of the soul is that lies have always been repugnant to me and the mere exaggeration of terms that almost everyone abuses, unconsciously, nowadays shocks me like a false note, a lack of harmony. My mother cannot imagine to what point she dug with her own hands the ditch that separated us all her life and made us such strangers to one another when she cried to me in her exaggerated voice, with regard to something trivial—dirty trousers or a little sweat moistening my forehead after a game—"Oh, wretched child, you'll make me die of chagrin!" Later, the adjectives *charming, delightful, adorable* and *ravishing*, employed by women in every sentence with regard to insignificant things, put me beside myself. Even the formulae of politeness, banal *How are yous?* on arrival, rang dolorously in my ears, so much did I sense that they rang false, and because it was always the most indifferent who seemed to be most keenly interested in your health. That was why I had conceived an esteem for the old pharmacist of Saint-Roch, simply because I had been told that, one day, an aged mealy-mouthed gossip having said on entering, "Bonjour Monsieur Guillaume, how are you?" he had replied brutally: "What can it matter to you?"

How, then, can I explain the need to invent that sometimes haunted me so imperiously that I came to tell stories, always false, to neighbors in an omnibus for no reason, simply for the pleasure of telling a lie; the need to betray the truth that ensured that between two indifferent stories, one true and one false, it was always the false one that I chose for preference, and which, by virtue of a singular mental phenomenon, which I can only observe without being able to explain it, seemed to me to be *truer than what had happened*—perhaps because it was more plausible and my mind, which has an invincible horror of the complicated, preferred to admit the lie as the veritable truth for the reason that it was simple, rather than the real truth, if it was complicated.

Is that not a commencement of a perturbation of mental being, disquieting because of its inevitable consequences? And is not that scission in the Self, that separation into two distinct beings, one of whom is impelled to lie—or, to be more exact, is vertiginously attracted by lying—while the other witnesses the lie as an impotent spectator and observer, listens to it, observes it, judges it and is scornful of it, an early symptom of the particular genre of dementia that I have been able to observe at Saint-Anne under the explicit denomination of "split personality"?

"Split personality" is still the observation of a fact and not its explanation. Physicians have always been great inventors of labels, only able to do that. They have not entered profoundly into any malady because they have only been able to observe *in anima vili*.

There is no difference between medicine and veterinary art. The responses of the patient deflect the physician more than they serve him, for the reason that almost all invalids cannot understand the question and cannot respond to it, and that those who could understand it, never having been able to take account of their functioning in a state of health, cannot take account of its morbid manifestations. They are the dupes of false sensations, which they express in words of which they often do not know the meaning or the scope. I shall always remember one patient who came to the free consultation of one of the physicians at the Charité, Doctor Laboulbène.[1] The habitual question: "What's wrong with you, my friend?" elicited this literal response: "I have something like an idea that fiddles with my head and descends into my stomach,

---

1 Joseph-Alexandre Laboulbène (1825-1898).

and comes back up worse, and recommences worse." No one could get anything else out of him.

Perhaps this monograph, if it came before the eyes of a competent individual, might open new horizons to him, but that consideration is of no value to me; no other eye than mine will ever penetrate the mystery. I need that certainty, in fact, in order to be able to lay my soul and my thought bare.

Is conscious madness frequent? That is a point on which, for fear of betraying myself, I have not dared to interrogate any of my masters or my comrades who are occupied with mental illness.

One sensation that is personal to me—at least, I believe so—is this one, on the curious aspect of which I have reflected at length, and of which I even believe that I have found in the end a sort of quasi-plausible explanation. I have experienced it twice in my life: it is, at the moment when one has just said or done something, the extraordinarily troubling sensation of having already said or done the same thing in exactly the same terms or circumstances.

For myself, I have in addition a very clear sensation of having lived before. I know where; it was in Bretagne. I have been a fisherman, no more than a hundred years ago.

How did that revelation of an anterior existence come to me? A few years ago, during my fifth-form vacation, I made a two-month excursion to Bretagne with friends. One evening, worn out by a trek of four or five leagues, given an appetite by the walk and the keen wind that was blowing from the coast, we arrived at Plougastel-Daoulas. We penetrated, a little noisily, into the sole inn in the locality, kept by a tall dark-haired woman whose haughty profile and harsh expression I can still see. Was she indisposed by our slightly cavalier intrusion? Did she have an apprehension of some indecent orgy? I don't know. At any rate, she absolutely refused to give us hospitality. But I remember perfectly that at the same time that I pronounced the sentence: "Come on, Madame Salaün, simply make us a *cotriate*, we'll be content with that," I recalled instantaneously that I had already pronounced the same sentence, in exactly the same circumstances, *before*. And I also remember the profound disturbance into which that reminiscence threw me.

"What's a cotriate?" one of my friends asked me.

"Well," I said, "as everyone ought to know, it's what people hereabouts call fish soup, isn't it Madame Salaün?"

The hostess nodded her head.

"You've been to Bretagne before, then?"

"Never."

"Then how do you know?"

I was nonplussed. In fact, how the devil did I know? And I repeated: *cotriate, cotriate*. A singular phenomenon: as I reflected and as I repeated the word, it lost its meaning; it ended up no longer representing anything to me, and I was obliged to observe that I had repeated it just like a parrot.

"Have you ever eaten it?"

I hesitated, on the point of saying yes; then, on reflection, I affirmed: "No, never."

My friends fell silent, renouncing understanding.

II

THEY did not understand either my sudden and intense emotion, an emotion that made me pale and left me impotent for quite a long time to utter a word before the bay of Douarnenez. The reason for that emotion was not, as they imagined, because I was violently under the charm of the delightful bay, so cheerful and gay, with such a luminously gray tint; no, it was because I had to admit to myself that none of the details of that vast and ravishing panorama were strange to me, that I had already had that spectacle before my eyes and that I had once sailed over those calm waters, so gently agitated by a languid and mild ripple.

In the boat that we had hired in order to sail in the bay, idling in the prow with my head in my hands and my eyes looking toward the horizon over the crests of little waves that were running over the sea like little white flames, I was pensive, huddled in a stubborn mutism that my companions respected, taking it for an admiring and entranced contemplation. I was attempting to struggle at close quarters with the haunting, obsessive idea that was anchored in my brain, hanging on with beak and fingernails, the idea that was unhinging me, that I was not a man like others, and that the sinuous and murky route of darkness in which I was going henceforth to agitate desperately, would lead to the roaring and turbulent maelstrom of madness.

The vessel's stem collided heavily with the waves, which were swelling, rolled by the breeze that was getting up, and sometimes splashed us, pouring noisily into the boat. My face was streaming, dusted with spray and whipped by the wind; and that sensation of damp, violently aromatic wind, was salutary; the cold shower reanimated me, recalled me to reason and extracted my analytical faculties from the depths where they were entangled. While the enormous red sail was inflated overhead and the mast and rigging creaked under the pressure of the wind, I persisted stubbornly in the search for an explanation of the recent phenomenon.

The idea of an anterior life, emitted above, is absurd. My reason rejected it. I searched for something else.

It is constantly observed that many vices are explained by heredity, the inexorable laws of atavism are beginning to be known. It is averred that manias, tics and habits, as well as diatheses, viruses and deformations, are inherited from a father or a grandfather. The gestural habit known as a tic is a muscular memory. Since the memory of the muscle is transmitted, why should the memory of the brain not also transmit the image of a location photographed by the memory. My great-grandfather, Jean Barban, with his determined zest for life, great lover of voyages that he was, might have visited Bretagne; perhaps the bay of Douarnenez had struck his imagination, and the image was profoundly engraved in his "gray matter." That image might then have been transmitted intact, reduced by a hundred millionth, in one of the nervous centers of the spermatozoon of which I am the issue. Perhaps it found its place in my brain when the moment came, and remained there, latent, lying in ambush, until the day when my voyage to the bay of Douarnenez made it surge forth. Is that not plausible? An analogous phenomenon must have been produced for the word *cotriate*, which my grandfather would have pronounced, and of which the print was conserved in his psyche.[1]

That theory has soothed me considerably. In addition, it has induced bitter conclusions regarding responsibility, conscience and human liberty. If the theory is admitted, how many singular and shocking prejudices and preconceived opinions could be explained. They would merely be inherited atavistic opinions.

I used the word *print* just now. But perhaps, the question being broadened, it can be applied to humans, to the species, in a general fashion, the uninterrupted succession of individuals being a series of

---

1 Léo Trézenik had lived in Brittany for some time when he was at the Jesuit college of Saint-François Xavier in Vannes and probably visited Douarnenez, in what might well have seemed to him by 1890 to have been a different life.

proofs taken of the same initial negative, destined to repeat in perpetuity the same phrases, to mull over the same ideas, to reproduce the same actions in identical circumstances, over a distance of millions of centuries.

Is the particular intelligence of animals that scholars call "instinct" anything other than memory? Instinct pushes them irresistibly to perform, in certain determined cases, certain defined actions. Thus, there is in coleoptera a very curious instinct that leads those insects, whose destiny is to die immediately after having produced, to deposit their eggs in a place where the larvae can nourish themselves. Monsieur Menault,[1] in his *Amour maternel chez les animaux*, says: "That foresight of posterity is remarkable in the coleopteran. The cockchafer, which only eats the leaves and seeds of the elm, could not live on roots, but the female buries her eggs in order that, when they hatch, the larvae are within range of the roots on which they, by contrast, must nourish themselves. Other female coleopterans heap up provisions around their eggs for the usage of a posterity that they cannot know, since they die before the birth of their larvae. Instinct tells the female insect where she ought to lay her eggs, and how she ought to assure the existence of her posterity, without it being possible to know whether she remembers what she ate herself in the larval state."

---

1 The zoologist Ernest Menault (1830-1903), author of *L'Intelligence des animaux* (1872) and *L'Amour maternel chez les animaux* (1874).

What is the "instinct" that indicates to the female insect where she should lay her eggs, if not what I called above "muscular memory," which is inscribed in all the muscles concurrent in the same function: memory transmitted by the muscles of one generation to the muscles of another, and which, mechanically, automatically—since no immediate necessity can impel them to act thus, enters into contraction at the appropriate moment.

Well, perhaps, in the same way, humans only think, act and speak by means of memory, all their movements being regulated in advance. Perhaps there are certain individuals who are the exact, identical, material reproduction of others that have existed before them. Perhaps, after the lapse of a certain revolution of years, the same actions are carried out again, the same words spoken again, the same events unfold and the same inventions, having been forgotten, are discovered again. Perhaps there are dead humanities, as there are engulfed lands, vanished cities, extinct peoples and finished races.

These general and retrospective considerations have distracted me momentarily from the hallucinatory preoccupation of my case, the aggravation of which it is necessary for me to observe day by day. And that observation I can only make before the impassive but cruelly revelatory mirror of this journal.

I am alone in the world. Alone! Not one heart to which to confide the atrocious distress of my soul. Not one mind, even among the most enlightened, that could comprehend this particular situation, this mental malady made of nuances and perhapses, imprecise, without emphatic symptoms. Have I not seen how physicians listen to the sick, with the prejudice of not hearing, not seeing and not believing that is built into their "yes, my friend"? Have I not, many a time, at Saint-Anne, heard distinguished alienists like Ball "reestablish the truth" for the pupils after a patient has told his story and "put them on guard" against the "false sensations" of which the latter is the dupe? *False sensations* is soon said. But what do they know? To me too, if I had the imprudence to take a physician—or anyone else—as a confident of my strange sensations, he would respond that they are false . . .

No, no confidences! Swallow your terror and digest it, if you can . . . !

And yet, how much good it would do me to be listened to, to be taken seriously, and for the narration of my tortures not to be greeted by a snigger and a shrug of the shoulders! But there is no one! I march isolated in life. The people I pass on the sidewalk are as foreign to me as if we did not speak the same language. What a relief even the philosophy of Abbé Desmares might have been! If I have ceased to see him; if I have fled him as a man in despair flees the joy of others, it is because his irony made me feel ill, because the superficiality of his comprehension of life exasperated me. I wanted him, and I still want him, not to have been able to see through me, to have by-passed my agony without even having suspected it.

I am alone!

Oh, if I could only encounter *her*, so long hoped for and awaited. Her, salvation! Her, the Beloved! If I encountered her, with what sincere joy, with what enthusiastic gratitude, I would murmur the strophes of *Arrière-saison*, a philosophy so indulgent and so fraternal, and so good . . . those verses moistened with tears that have made me weep so many times and so many times have warmed up my poor chilled soul with their welcoming morality, so magnificently human![1]

Oh, Coppée, my poet, Coppée, the most human and truest of poets, how one senses that you have suffered in the past! And what a delight to read the pages, so simply and delectably emotional, of *Arrière-saison*, in which your soul vibrates and sobs in every verse! Oh, yes how I would say to the poor beloved, somewhat broken by life:

Alas, why I have I encountered you so late,
Rose of my autumn, O adored darling,
Why, why so late?

And when her poor little heart swelled at the memory of her execrated past, how quickly I would console her:

1 The sequence of poems entitled "Arrière-saison," by François Coppée (1842-1908), was first published as a small book by Alphonse Lemerre in 1887, and reprinted the following year in the author's *Oeuvres complètes*. When Trézenik's family first moved to Paris they lived in the same apartment building as Coppée.

You have not always been good,
You whose heart is beating on my arm.
For more than one passing lover
You smiled and you sighed.

In a shameful and grim voice
You told me that one blue evening;
But my mouth closed your mouth,
Which purified your confession.

I had foreseen your confession,
I had divined your story,
Imprudent daughter of the people
Who no longer had a mother.

In May, under the meager foliage,
The suburban sparrows sang,
Didn't they? The vague ennui, the age . . . ?
I know those sad amours.

But the heart to which you cling,
Having suffered, is able to excuse;
And I see in your sincere eyes
That I have your first sincere kiss.

Of the two of us, you are the better,
Since you know better how to love.
Look, my child, I'm weeping,
Me, so blasé, and already so old.

For the tender and simple manner
With which you have confessed your past,
I owe you my last tear
And by that it is effaced.

But no. *She* will not come, she will never come! I am alone. I shall remain alone . . .

I shall always be alone, in any case, always; I have never found sympathy in the true and complete meaning of the word. Thus, I acquired very young the habit of keeping everything to myself, of not saying anything of what I thought and what happened to me, good or bad. Later, a confidence always cost me, even on the rare occasions when it was cheerful. All the more reason why it is impossible for me to open up today with regard to my misfortune, since I have an even greater certainty of not being understood.

And yet, any confession is a relief. That is so true that my anguish is less intense since I have commenced this confession for myself, for myself alone. Any peril boldly envisaged is lessened. And then, such is my nature that I have always, I repeat, suffered more from the anticipation and uncertainty of an evil than from the evil itself. I will even add that I have always had a tendency to anxiety. But in recent times that tendency has been magnified. I even fear that my will, once so clear, so firm and so vibrant, might be afflicted.

I have observed that for a month or two—and I had never observed it before—I have experienced great difficulty in leaving my apartment. It seems to me that I have forgotten something. I mark time, I turn back, I search, I go from one room to another, I tap my pocket to make sure that the familiar objects are really there, I ascertain that nothing is missing . . . and I can't decide to leave. It has happened that I remain, in those circumstances, so painful is the sensation that I have forgotten something important. But what is singular is that it appears that the something in question is not an object but a part of myself; it seems to me that I am not entire. That is why it is painful to go out, and that, sometimes, rather than separate myself from that portion of myself, I remain.

That anxiety has recently taken on another form.

Climbing the steep staircase of the Vincennes railway station, in the midst of the crowd taking the trains to Joinville and Comte-Robert, it seemed to me—this was about a week ago—that mocking eyes were staring at me and that people were nudging one another and winking with amusement in my direction. I stopped and let the crowd pass, sitting on a banquette. Then, timidly, I extended my hand, with the apprehension of encountering a hitch in the ridiculous and visible part of my trousers. Nothing! Absolutely nothing! The fabric was intact. The sniggers, therefore, were not destined for me. But fear had been born within me, an absurd and obsessive fear, a fear that now no longer lets go of me, a fear that I cannot vanquish, a fear that paralyzes me and makes me awkward every time I see people below me, a stupid fear that my trousers have ripped without me being aware of it, and that an opening is gaping *there*, in the grotesque place. And the terror of being laughed at by everyone, the object of sarcastic whispers, the focal point of gazes, grips me, invades me, dominates me and hypnotizes me . . .

And, pale with anxiety, the obsession no longer quitting me, I ask myself: "What do I do if that happens to me? What do I do if, suddenly, on the railway in the middle of the street, or going up to the top deck of an omnibus, that dreaded rip—and it will come, I'm sure of it—happens?" I have already noted my insurmountable fear of ridicule. Now, what is more ridiculous than a man who is sporting a gaping hole *there*? Yes, what can I do? Wear a coat with tails? I have a horror of such garments—and in any case, the tails can part. Besides which, it's too uncomfortable in summer. What to do . . . ?

I've found the answer. I go out now with a little package under my arm, which reassures me and returns calm and tranquility to my mind: a little package that never leaves me, a little package—this is another thing that imbecilic alienists wouldn't understand and which would make them shrug their superior shoulders—wrapped in newspaper and carefully tied with string, which contains a spare pair of trousers.

III

THE quarter in which I live today, the Place Daumesnil, is a bleak quarter, and that is why I chose it and I love it. In five minutes I can wander under the thick verdure of the Bois de Vincennes, parading my melancholy on the bank of its lakes, stop abruptly before the sudden and unexpected vision of a charming location which reposes my eye. I have only to descend the Avenue Dumesnil and I bump into workmen in blue blouses with features hardened by relentless quotidian labor and housewives in curlers coming down from their fifth-floor apartment in order to have a chat with the maid opposite under the plane trees of the avenue.

It would be impossible for me to live in the populous quarters. I no longer have the philosophy necessary to go past impassively all those stupid faces that throng the sidewalks, to hear all those loud stupidities that splash you in passing, all the snatches of stupid conversations that lash you in the face like the thong of a whip and raise the blood like a slap. On the rare occasions when I have risked myself in

Paris I have come back clenched by a kind of rage, the outbursts of which I have all the trouble in the world containing, and which sometimes erupt involuntarily in ill-sounding epithets that alarm the strollers, rudely jostled and grumbling. Commonplaces, clichés, ready-made phrases and accepted stupidities: that alone composes the fragments of dialogue heard everyday at the hazard of the sidewalks, on omnibuses, on railways trains in the foyers of theaters, and all the places where crowds stagnate or circulate.

Banal ideas and ready-made phrases, isn't that what provides the foundations of books and newspapers? I've got to the point of no longer reading. The last time that printed lines passed before my eyes was in the illustrated supplement of some daily. I remember it. There were three short stories; and the three authors, having to depict the blue eyes of a woman, all compared them, originally, to the blue of a forget-me-not. Three forget-me-nots in a single day in a single newspaper is two too many—and perhaps three. I no longer read. In any case, reading requires too much effort. I can no longer concentrate my thought, just as I can no longer find the formula of any idea other than by writing it down. Thus, my journal has become an imperious and quotidian necessity.

The immediate consequence of the cloistered and isolated life that I lead is the hypochondria into which I feel myself sinking further every day: a black, grim hypochondria which could easily become peevish but which is not without charm. I no longer experience the need to formulate my thought, much less to address a few banal words to one of those cretins whom the irony of words describes as my fellows. Nothing in life interests me any longer, and in truth, I don't know why I don't kill myself.

Perhaps the only thing that attaches me to life is the singular and cruel interest that I end up taking in dissecting myself like this, fiber by fiber, in analyzing myself, watching myself act, listening to myself thinking, criticizing myself and blaming myself for my actions. For the strange phenomenon of duplication that I have been obliged to recognize in myself several times is taking on troubling proportions. I can presently observe in myself, quite clearly, two individuals, absolutely different in essence, with diametrically opposite tastes: one that acts and another that criticizes the action; one that formulates an opinion and another that shrugs his shoulders and murmurs aloud, with my voice: "Imbecile!"

That sensation of being two people is very annoying. There are sometimes dialogues and arguments. One wants one thing, and the other says to him: "That's idiotic; you won't do it." The first has arrived at doing certain things out of simple perversity, to irritate the other.

That dualism and its analysis are the sole consolation of my increasing hypochondria.

I imagine, however, that this dualism, which is unhealthily exaggerated in me, must exist, moderated and coordinated, in all intellectuals. The multiplicity of the self has not yet been thoroughly studied. It is evident that every litterateur is double; there is the producer and the critic. Sometimes—often—the producer is predominant and the critic is annihilated, unable to make himself heard, seeing his voice stifled. How many modern works have no other explanation! When there is equilibrium, when one judges the other without acrimony, the work is at ease, pondered; that makes great talents in all literatures; but when the critic is implacable, when only his voice makes itself heard, the producer is impotent; that produces the discouraged individuals who tear up the page when it is scarcely terminated. It is in that category that I would be placed if I had, as they say, "made literature."

One of the results of the constant and stubborn psychic auto-vivisection that has become the principal occupation of my life is what I shall call, for want of more exact terms, the hyperesthesia of my imagination. I have already noted the tendency that I have sometimes to confound dream and reality under certain influences of temperature and light, principally during the hour that precedes sunset, at the particular moment, gripping for all sensitive individuals, that painters have justly dubbed "the moment of the effect." Nowadays my overexcited imagination has become so excessive in its impressionability that I can no longer think that something might happen without one of my two selves imagining that it has happened, and suffering and despairing as if it had happened, while the other sniggers and teases, and calls the other a simpleton and an imbecile.

The day before yesterday I was on my fifth-floor balcony, my eyes on the bitumen of the causeway, when an apprehension was suddenly formulated within me: perhaps the grille was not very solid; if it suddenly gave way I would be precipitated into the air and would crash on to the sidewalk. At the same instant I had a very clear sensation that the ironwork had come away and that I was spinning in mid-air, my arms in a cross; an atrocious oppression gripped my throat, the oppression of a rapid fall; at one point I even perceived people who were seeing me fall; I heard their cry of "Oh my God!" and suddenly, I experienced a shock, the violence of which robbed me instantaneously of all sentiment; my temples were buzzing, as if an entire river had been precipitated into my ears; I did not experience any pain, I felt annihilated, as if rid of my body, and my brain devoid of thought, bathed in a sort of misty penumbra . . . When I came to I was lying on the balcony, where the violence of the sensation had caused me to faint.

Those alarms of my imagination increasingly escape the direction of my will. I can observe their progress every week. I am still able to recognize the chimerical nature of the visions that now haunt me every evening, but, almost mathematically, I could determine the day when my faculty of control will be annihilated, when I will be the irresponsible and disorientated dupe of my Chimera. But what chimera? I don't know yet. My brain, where the fog trails, can engender any of them, and I sense that my arm might equip itself for the worst murders . . .

But today, still, I know, I can certify that the hallucinations populating the darkness of my nights are hallucinations. Better informed, rid of fear, without terror of the unknown and the invisible, I can see, hear, look, observe, take note and interest myself. But I'm no longer afraid. It's necessary to say that if my childhood knew habitual hallucinations of hearing and sight, I have been able, in recent times, to observe in myself the rare hallucinations of smell, taste and touch.

The curious aspect of those chimeras is that they depart from me, that they emerge from my brain, that I witness their hatching and that I see them emerging, save for one, always the same, that comes from outside and which comes back every evening.

Everyone does not go to sleep in the same fashion. Some pass abruptly, without transition, from wakefulness to slumber. In others, those two states are separated by an intermediate state that I call the twilight of dreams, during which, all the great faculties being already torpid, while consciousness and imagination are not, the latter is abandoned to itself and delivers itself with impunity to all its fantasies. Then, a host of more or less fantastic figures files before the inner gaze, which becomes one of the elements of the dreams to come. In me, it does not happen at all as in the first instance, and not entirely as in the second.

One of my two selves goes to sleep first, and the other watches it go to sleep, but the second is the imaginative self, nervous and impressionable. It takes pleasure in the frequentation of hallucinations and evokes them if necessary. Then, during the moment that I call the twilight of dreams, freed from all control, once the other is asleep, it invites all the chimeras of its meninges to "get some air." They emerge one by one, and in the bedroom, by the glow of the night-light, there is an infernal saraband, by which I am no longer frightened, as in my childhood, because I know the point of departure and I know where all those phantoms have come from.

But suddenly—and it is here that I almost begin to become anxious, for what follows is independent of my will—the door of my bedroom, which I lock carefully every evening, rotates slowly and silently on its hinges, and an apparition comes in, before which the phantoms that populate the darkness melt away and vanish like shadows fleeing before the sun: a woman; or, rather, a girl.

I have had the time to examine her, since I have seen her every evening for more than a month. She is tall and slim and her blue gaze, atrociously sad—so sad that every time I see her I am gripped, as I gaze at her, by a stifling anguish—her blue gaze stops in passing, lingering upon me; she glides to the back of the room, sits down in an armchair a long way from the night-light, and starts to weep. And for long hours I *hear* her tears rolling down her cheeks. As soon as dawn blanches the curtains imperceptibly and makes the night-light pale, the sad Visitor goes away.

One evening, the temptation came to me to get up and take her in my arms in order to console her, but it was impossible for me to make a movement. My legs and my arms were inert, as if some mysterious scalpel had operated within me to section the motor nerves.

I wondered whether, on this occasion, I was once again the victim of a hallucination engendered by my sick brain or whether *She* really existed. All the recent experiments of Doctor Crookes, about which all the Institutes are caviling at present, give me the right to believe in that existence, but my reason opposes it.[1] My reason! Can I still base myself on that? My reason! Do I still have the right to retrench myself behind that rampart?

I ruminated for an entire day regarding some conclusive experiment that could bring me a conviction in one direction or the other. I attempted one, and the result cast me into a great disturbance.

She came; her gaze, moistened by tears, reposed on mine with an infinite sadness and her tears commenced flowing again; anguish and dolor compressed my lungs so violently that it seemed to me that all respiration ceased within me.

"How I'm suffering!" I murmured, internally—for my oppression was such that I would not have been able to articulate a word—"and what an ardent thirst is burning me!"

She had raised her eyes, and slowly paraded her dolorous gaze around her.

I continued: "I have limbs broken by fatigue; it seems to me that life has withdrawn from them; I can't drag myself over there as far as the glass of

---

1 William Crookes' lectures on and supposed demonstrations of the phenomena of Spiritualism, including one before the skeptical members of the Royal Society in the late 1870s, were widely reported, often wildly exaggerated, and became something of a *cause célèbre* in France.

water on my mantelpiece, and I have a furnace in my throat . . ."

She had risen to her feet. She took the glass in her left hand while the right tilted the neck of the carafe above it; and I saw distinctly the water pass from one to the other, and I heard the glug-glug of the liquid. Then she advanced toward my bed and her shadow was interposed between her and the night-light; I no longer saw anything but a confused mass, from which a sweet and penetrating odor emanated, which it was impossible for me to identify.

I could no longer see anything, but I heard . . . yes, I heard, distinctly, the word "Drink!" murmured in my ear by a soft voice . . . and I felt . . . first of all a warm hand that slid under my head, then, suddenly, the cold contact of the glass on my lips and the freshness of the flowing water . . . I felt it! No, no, I was the dupe of an illusion . . . And I also heard, beside me, quite clearly, *her* respiration, very regular, suddenly interrupted by a long sigh that almost resembled a lamentation. And I was invaded by a languor so delicious, I felt myself cradled, with the breath of breezes around the forehead, in a bliss so supraterrestrial that it appeared to me that I no longer had a body and that I was a spirit floating in the glaucous ether of celestial space . . .

It was only the next day that the reflections of the awakening threw me into all the pangs of terror, and that the certainty that I was going mad imposed itself again on my mind, more obsessive and more anguishing than it had ever been.

IV

NEW troubles have become manifest within me. Now I experience the greatest difficulty in speaking. I have in my throat something like a dolorous claw, which prevents my larynx from contracting and entering into vibration. It's necessary for me to lift a mountain in order to pronounce a single word; so I no longer pronounce any but indispensable words; my voice frightens me; I no longer recognize it, it has a broken, veiled, tremulous timbre; it really sounds cracked, and when, by chance, I emit a sound in the solitude of my apartment, the sound vibrates so singularly in the emptiness of the rooms, and rolls and fractures so strangely at the angles of the furniture, that I turn round, as if it were someone else who had spoken.

And, in fact, it must be another. I perceive that I never say what I wanted to say, what I had formulated internally. The timbre of that voice is not the one to which my ears are accustomed and the phrase pronounced does not belong to me, has not emerged from my brain. Another is making use of my lungs to blow air into my larynx and contract the muscles of my tongue, and the phrase spoken does not express my thought. There are days when that foreign influence is so manifest that I need to collect the scattered fragments of my will in order to resist it. And exasperations take hold of me, fits of anger and terrible rage against the Being that is interposing itself so perversely between the order of my will and its execution . . . fits of anger that might drive me to murder. I shall kill *it*. That would not be a suicide, it would be an assassination . . .

Was it yesterday or was it a week ago? I'm losing the notion of time. There are weeks that stretch out like months, and others that disappear, with holes, as if Saturday had suddenly become juxtaposed with Monday. Was it yesterday? I think so. I went out for my favorite walk through the shady thickets of the Bois de Vincennes. I was going down the Avenue Daumesnil when I saw Costelle going past in a fiacre, at the trot, with a woman. And I thought: *He hasn't seen me; so much the better; I 'm determined not to see him again.*

But the Other couldn't miss such a fine opportunity to play a joke on me. He made grand gestures with my arms. And I muttered: "But I don't want to see Costelle; I shan't say a word to him." And I advanced toward the coachman, who had noticed the appeals of my arms. "It's idiotic," I continued monologuing, ill-humoredly, "I'm going to say disagreeable things." But the Other had brought me in a few strides close to Costelle, who uttered wholly southern exclamations.

And against my will my mouth murmured, in the hoarse voice that *he* found on such occasions: "How glad I am to see you again, my dear friend, how have you been since . . ."

However, while Costelle shook my hand effusively, inviting me to take a place beside him in the carriage in order to make a tour of the wood, I succeeded in regaining possession of myself with a violent effort that must have contracted my face bizarrely, for I perceived that Costelle's companion was looking at me with a fearful expression, and I replied, or rather I howled, in a furious voice: "I'm walking on my own, you're disturbing me." And, emphasizing the effort commenced, I fled at a run.

Hostilities have opened between Him and Me. I say Him and Me, although it is really Me and Me, because it expresses my thought better. It is now a perpetual struggle in which I can only be the victor on condition of being always alert, of not having a single distraction—and He seeks to provide me with them—and always having one eye open on Him.

Thus far He has only had Sensibility and Imagination on his side, which is a great deal, but I have Reason and Judgment on mine; I still hold the helm of the Will, of which, from time to time, by virtue of a distraction, he snatches the tiller from my hand. But I seize the upper hand again. It happens, though, that He hangs on to the helm at the same time as me; on those days, the Beast, without direction, goes wherever his instincts push him, and revels.

Thus, one evening, I found myself in the depths of a dive to which the Animal had taken both of us while we were battling, and from which we returned with a common shame and disgust. But it's very rare that we encounter one another in a common opinion and an action. One would think, on the contrary, that his sole concern is to inform himself of my needs in order to prevent me from satisfying them, and of my desires in order to thwart them. I have all the difficulty in the world now in going where I want to go. I leave for the wood every day after breakfast; *he* knows my mania, and there are the same perverse machinations every time. He takes me on to the sidewalk that winds around the fountain of the Place Dumesnil. That circular sidewalk draws me astray, the monumental lions that spit into the stucco bowl lead my thought far away, and when I get a grip on myself again I find myself in the process of going along the Avenue Dumesnil in the direction of the Bastille.

It's necessary that I weigh the words that I'm about to pronounce, that I turn them over my tongue seven times, as the popular saying has it; otherwise, having gone to stationer's with the formal intention of acquiring a box of pens, it's a box of espadrilles that I ask for, glad when my lips haven't articulated a few insulting or obscene words.

But it isn't limited to words. It has happened to me to fly into childish tantrums, accompanied by foot-stamping and inarticulate cries, hammering on doors with my fists and breaking vases that I was holding—and it was always those that I treasure most that I broke, or, rather, which *he* made me break—and that for a detail devoid of importance, a bagatelle, a futility, nothing at all . . . And in those moments, I'm capable of killing . . . yes, of killing . . .

V

A further interruption of a year. And how many events in that year! How many events that have, if not overturned my existence completely, at least given it a new and quite different orientation.

A year without touching this journal, which I once declared indispensable to my intellectual health: a calm year. A cessation in the progress of the malady, perhaps a cure.

A cure!

To begin with, my mother is dead. And I write that without a tear; I conducted her to her final abode without a tear.

Abbé Desmares, whom I was obliged to see again on that occasion, tried to penetrate me with the aid of clever questions, but he could not find any issue by which to slide into my matured soul. His gaze fixed itself on mine with an anxious amazement.

"Something grave is happening in you, Marie-Joseph," he said to me, sadly, "something of which you aren't taking account . . . and perhaps you're going toward a gulf . . . from which I might be able to save you if you had confidence me, as you once did, and if you dared to open your thought to me a little . . ." And as I remained silent, obstinate in an almost hateful mutism, the priest concluded, as he quit me: "I won't tell you everything that I have in my heart, but I'm afraid, my poor child, I'm very afraid for you."

That appeal remained without an echo. Have all the wellsprings of sensibility dried up within me, then? I believe so, and I repeated to myself, bitterly, while returning from Saint-Roch, when the affairs of the succession were terminated—I have confided the care of my interests to the notary of Saint-Roch, leaving him the right to direct my little fortune as he wishes, provided that he sends me the income regularly—that I believed that all the living forces of my being had reverted to my brain, that my heart had ossified fiber by fiber, and that nothing any longer vibrated within me . . .

I believed that until I encountered Germaine . . .

There is a woman in my life! And a woman who fills it to such a point that I forget myself, that my brain has been de-hypnotized of its obsession, that hope has returned to me; that I dare to write the word *madness* without trembling, almost without believing it; that it seems to me that I have got a grip on myself entirely again because she is there, that the rustle of her dress has chased away the black devils, that the grace of her smile and the soft gleam of her blue eyes has melted the darkness of my soul, and that she illuminates my life as if a dawn rises before her at every step she takes!

Oh, in order to write that story, her story, with what joy I have finally taken up this pen again, to which I had feared momentarily that my fingers had become dishabituated.

Singularly enough, since *She* has been here, the Other has abruptly ceased his mischief-making. I am alone, I am one, I am free, I can want what I like, say what I want to say and do what I want to do. *He* has shut up. He gives no sign of existence. I can speak without my voice frightening me, I can look into a mirror without it sending me back a convulsed face in which, recently, I had thought I recognized a commencement of asymmetry, and without my anxious gaze fleeing the fixity of my dilated pupils.

I had returned from Saint-Roch . . . how long ago was it? It's singular, but it's impossible for me to be precise in that regard. The days melt away now, with a rapidity so inconceivable that it sometimes seems to me that the moment of getting up and the moment of going to bed have no separation. I have not retained any memory of anything. If my stomach does not protest I could affirm that I have neither breakfasted nor dined.

Entire weeks—but are they really weeks—disappear without me being able to note a single event on which my memory can fix. I have lost the notion of time, as I have lost the meaning of certain words, especially words that do not have a Latin or Greek etymology.

The time, the inappreciable lapse of time—weeks or months—that has gone by since my arrival from

Saint-Roch passed like a dream. I remember suddenly that during my year of philosophy I was ill, with a singular malady that almost made me withdraw from the college. I imagined, following the example of Berkeley, that the phenomena of nature or the soul were only ideas in the mind; that the external world, tangible objects as well as visible objects, do not exist outside the mind. But, said the adversaries of the theory, when you receive a blow on the arm, the pain informs you and demonstrates to you that your body really exists. To that I responded: when I dream, while asleep, that I receive a blow on the arm, I howl as if I had received it, and yet I have not received it. Thus, that proof does not prove anything. Thus, I have no right to conclude that anything exists but thought, and everything that seems to me to be outside me is nothing but appearances, ideas in my brain. And that aberration tortured me for some three months.

It has come back since, as vivid and as anguishing, although not of such long duration. It came back, as I noted just now, on the very day of my mother's burial. It is through a sort of fog, sufficiently analogous to the fog of drunkenness, that I see myself again walking behind the hearse to the church, where I can hear the sad intoning of psalms of death, and, following the custom, I shake the hands of many people at the exit from the cemetery—a burlesque and interminable file, squeezing hard enough to make me cry out—whose faces my tranquil and imperceptible ironic gaze scrutinize in passing, reading the indifference under the sadness of attitude and the circumstantial grimace. It is in that fog that I lived until *Her* coming. But how did *She* come to me?

One evening in May, or perhaps April, the wind was whistling under my door a plaint so mournful that I resolved to go out in order to escape the anguish that was invading me. Dusk was falling. Already, along the Avenue Daumesnil, the street lights were coming on one by one. The Animal led me directly to the wood, without my having given him the slightest indication in that direction, and the *Other*, a detail that struck me, I remember, let go.

The wood was absolutely solitary; above my head the foliage was agitating with a little rattle. The Animal, whom with a sort of tacit agreement we abandoned to himself, marched straight to the lake, on which the reflection of black thickets was trembling like a sepia drawing. I sat down on a bench and fixed myself in the immobility of a statue, my ears lulled by the crackling of the foliage.

From time to time, the horn of a tram wept a guttural appeal that broke into my reverie. Gradually, night had fallen. The wood was pitch dark, and then it was suddenly illuminated. The moon had just emerged abruptly from a cloud and made a near-clarity under the leaves because of the lake, which served it as a reflector.

That pale brightening of the water and the verdure gave such a particular tint to the landscape that it seemed to me to be a hundred leagues from Paris, in some valley of Armorica haunted by gnomes and kor-rigans. I pricked up my ears instinctively, as if to listen to the dull impact of the laundry-beaters' clubs, and my gaze slowly made a tour of the lake, prepared at any moment to encounter some crouching silhouette . . . It stopped suddenly and became fixed . . .

In the distance, far away, in the gap between two shivering poplars, I had seen a black form move . . .

I hid myself as best I could in the shelter of a tall clump of spindle-trees, and darted my gaze, without any emotion, simply with interest, at what I saw—or thought I saw; for perhaps, after all, it was nothing but a bush stirred by the wind. No, definitely, it was really someone. The black form was now gliding over the grass and approaching me. The moon suddenly illuminated it as it traversed a path. It was a woman. It was impossible for me to distinguish anything of her face at the distance where she was from me; I could only observe that she had a disordered gait and appeared to be prey to the most violent despair. She sometimes took a few deliberate steps toward the lake, and then stopped, her arms extended, her hands turned back, with a torsion of terror, toward her neck.

Suddenly, she advanced to the water's edge, very close, rummaged in her pocket, pulled out her handkerchief and tied it solidly around her ankles; then she drew herself up to her full height, veiled her face with her hands and let herself fall . . . But, attentive to all her movements, I was behind her, and, before she had even brushed the water with her dress, I harpooned her with a vigorous wrist . . .

To the cry of fright that she uttered on feeling herself so unexpectedly snatched from suicide and transported to the nearby bench, I responded with a cry of amazement. She resembled, to such an extent as to unhinge my tottering reason completely, the hallucinatory visitor, the mysterious apparition of my feverish nights, the inexplicable phenomenon on which my disequilibrated thought no longer dared to dwell, by virtue of apprehension of the madness to which such preoccupations inevitably lead.

(And—I note this detail in haste in order not to come back to it—since She has been here, the Apparition has not returned!)

Whether or not she read in my gaze the sudden and irresistible sympathy that she inspired in me— the gaze that could not be detached from her eyes, her blue eyes, very soft, very tender and very profound; the eyes of the Apparition—she told me immediately that her name was Germaine, and that she was very unhappy, so unhappy that she had preferred to die rather than go on living.

And with a complete abandon, she told me her story.

The night was mild, the breeze was no longer blowing, the leaves fell silent in order to listen, the moonlight was streaming over the lake, absolutely motionless now, only wrinkled by the wake of a large white swan . . .

VI

SHE was born in Reims. She had been happy until the age of twelve, her parents having a good
understanding and each working for their part. Then
the father began to drink and the household fell into
poverty; the overworked mother fell ill. She suffered
for a long time from a terrible interior malady that
undermined her, and which she did not admit; it was
necessary to work and it was better to pay the baker
than the doctor.

When Germaine reached the age of fifteen her
mother died. What chagrin! And what an atrocious
sense of isolation gripped her when she returned to
the dead house alone, her father having stayed out
drinking with friends—to "drown his pain," he said.
A year passed, painfully. She was reduced, every
Saturday, to beg from her father's employer in order to
be able to eat during the week. As soon as his dinner
was swallowed the fellow would lock his daughter in
and run to the café. He only came back at night, beating the walls, and his daughter sometimes heard him
collapse in his room, where he snored on the floor

until morning, while she wept under her sheets, out of fear, shame and despair.

With what joy, therefore, and what gratitude, she welcomed a proposition to come and join her made one morning by a friend established and married in Paris, who offered her a place as cashier in her establishment.

What disillusionment! There were six months of that; but almost immediately she perceived that it was the role of a "maid of all work" that the friend reserved for her, harshly making her understand that she was at her discretion, that she did not know any métier, that she was not "streetwise" enough to get out of difficulty and that she ought to "deem herself fortunate" to be accepted without wages, for food.

For three months she swallowed her nausea. Then, one day, the husband had made her understand, brutally, that he found her pretty, and she was obliged to quit the house, to enter almost immediately into another, still in the quality of maid, after having tried to present herself as a sales clerk in one of the large fashion stores of Paris.

There again her prettiness had been fatal; the employee charged with recruiting staff had said to her, smiling, on the point of signing the engagement: "But you know, darling, that there's a preliminary condition to your admission into the house?"

"What's that?" the young woman asked, naïvely.

The store clerk got up, came close to her—very close—and murmured, which chucking her under the chin: "Well, it'll be necessary to sleep with me."

Since then, dragging her beauty like a cannonball, she had passed through half a dozen Parisian households, disgust on her lips, prickling with gooseflesh, soiled by lascivious frictions, splashed with furtive kisses, until, from one sickening to another and one nausea to another she had arrived at throwing herself into suicide as into a liberation.

We were going slowly up the Avenue Daumesnil as she finished that heart-rending story; she stopped walking abruptly and said to me, suddenly suspicious:

"But where are you taking me? And why have I told you all that? And why didn't you let me die?"

I responded, more to her thought than her speech:

"I know, as you do, what it is to be alone, absolutely alone in the world. Like you I've been obsessed for a long time by the idea of a liberating death. And this very evening I might have put into execution my long-determined design to finish with an existence that weighs upon me because it is devoid of joy, interest and affection. How is it that, having decided to die for my own account, I interposed myself between your resolution and its execution? I don't know. But while you were talking to me, the hope came to me that the addition of our two miseries might perhaps result in a little happiness . . ."

She did not say anything, her luminous eyes staring into mine.

"Oh, if only it were possible for you to have confidence in me!" I continued. "Don't you sense, don't you see anything that indicates to you that it's a friend who is speaking to you, perhaps a friend long hoped for . . ."

159

In a slow, pensive voice, she pronounced:

"Yes, there's a soft light in your eyes . . . yes, I feel attracted to you . . . It's singular, it seems to me that your voice isn't unknown to me, that I've heard it before, that I've seen you before, that I've known you for a long time, that I've found you again and that I recognize you, although I've only known you for an hour. Wait a moment while I try to remember . . . Yes, that's it, I've seen you in a dream, I see you every night . . . yes, it's really you, that's why I recognize you . . ."

"For how long?" I asked, very pale, thinking that it was for three months that the Apparition that resembled her so much had been coming to visit me every night."

"Three months," she replied. "And my dream is always the same . . . You're in bed in a large room that I've never been in, it's dark; I come in, but you remain motionless. Oh, I'd like so much that you'd come to meet me . . . I try to speak, to tell you my chagrins, but my lips are sealed by an invincible force; I can only weep, and I weep . . . until morning, until the awakening, and I get up, exhausted . . ."

It was true, then! It was her! Her dream, like mine, was a strange and inexplicable reality! I decided not to persist, not to seek to fathom it, sensing that the slightest shock might be irreparably deadly to the fissures in my brain through which my poor disorganized reason was filtering, drop by drop . . .

She was leaning on my arm now, inclining her long flexible figure slightly. We emerged into the Place Daumesnil, absolutely deserted at that hour, with its sparse flickering gas-lamps and its great glaucous lions, crouching with their heads high, motionless and majestic guardians, around the silent fountain, with its bleak houses, devoid of shops, its mute houses with extinct windows, and the somber border of its broad deserted avenues, reminiscent of some forum of a dead city abandoned by civilization . . .

Germaine had not spoken for some time; then she murmured:

"I'm very tired! Oh, yes, very tired . . . Oh, how nice it would have been back there, in the depths of the black water!"

I pointed to the balcony that was facing us, on the fifth floor of the corner house; and I said:

"That's where your friend lives. Would you like him to offer you a fraternal hospitality?"

Her long blue gaze fixed itself on mine again; I thought I could read a vague interrogation there that she did not formulate. I added:

"We'll discuss it tomorrow."

She simply said:

"I accept, my friend."

How singular all that is! And with what shrugs of the shoulders those confidences would be greeted by serious men, if they were to learn that it was on the edge of a lake streaming with moonlight into which she was about to throw herself romantically, as in the third act of a melodrama, that I encountered for the first time the only being that I have loved in the world, the Savior Soul that attaches me to life and might perhaps extract me from the horrors of madness, as I have extracted her from the annihilation of suicide . . .

VII

OUR little life is installed, very gently and very simply. My drawing room, slightly transformed, has become Germaine's bedroom. At first she was very reluctant to accept a definitive hospitality.

"By what title and by what right?" she said to me. "And how would your concierge regard me?"

I no longer know what explanation—very complicated, at any rate—I gave the concierge. No matter. The essential thing is that she acted with perfect tact. Nevertheless, in protest at my "immorality," the worthy woman pretends not to see Germaine, never mentions her to me, and when I remark that she has forgotten to set a place for "Madame" she sets one without saying a word, darting an astonished glance in my direction. But that concierge has always been strange. It's true that she is habituated to silence with me; I warned her, when taking her into my service, that I do not like observations or interrogations, that gossip is odious to me, and any loquaciousness very disagreeable. She took that as read. I don't believe that I've exchanged three words with her in the twelve or fifteen months that she has been in my service. Her attitude toward Germaine is merely the consequence of her rigorous respect for my orders. She knows that it is forbidden to her, if not to be astonished, at least to manifest her astonishment, and what she does not understand she rolls around in her obtuse brain but does not formulate. Can I ask for anything else?

I am no longer the same man since I have been in love with her. For I'm in love! I'm in love! I'm in love! I haven't told her yet; I don't want to tell her for a long time; our situation has so many charms. We're two lovers who are walking under the cover of a pretty little path carpeted with moss, which snakes, tortuous and full of birdsong, through the countryside, and we don't know where it leads. We don't know and we don't want to know. In the evening, I conduct her gravely to her bedroom door, and with a very eighteenth-century reverence—we give the impression of dancing a minuet—I say to her "Good night, Mademoiselle," and she responds to me in her pretty clear and fresh voice: "Good evening, Monsieur," and we burst out laughing. How charming it is!

How long will it last?

It's necessary that it lasts, for this amour is the best treatment, the only one, that can hinder the progress of my malady and, perhaps—the hope has returned to me now—to lead to a cure. I must have, very recently, confessed to her a part of the truth, admitted to her that I was ill, and that my cure was in her hands, in the joy of her smile and the soothing magnetism of her gaze. I must have told her because she has manifested her intention—firmly determined, she said—to work! I've revealed to her that my notary serves me with enough income for us to live in peace. In fact, that income has been noticeably augmented recently, the notary having found, he told me, an advantageous placement. And I concluded: "Work quite simply for our happiness." And, more quietly, in a tremulous voice: "Work for my cure; it's almost complete; don't abandon me."

"Ah!" she said, stammering slightly and blushing deeply, the darling. "You addressed me informally."

I remained, in truth, more emotional than her, and I muttered, awkwardly, a murky explanation from which she finally disengaged me by means of a burst of laughter.

Ah, that laughter is salvation!

Weeks have gone by. I am courting her! It's very funny. I bring wit into play, and unfamiliar gallantries. Her ingenuousness is an uncommon spice; and her sudden blushes, and the languor or gleam of her eyes, in which her naïve and new soul is reflected, is guiding me reliably toward the conquest of that confident little heart. And while all the forces of my thinking and sensational being converge toward that goal, the anguish of mounting madness relaxes its strangling grip a little and lets me breathe.

Oh, certainly, I no longer believed that I was susceptible to such an idyll. What month is it? I no longer know. All I know is that there are leaves on the trees and birds in the foliage, flowers in the hedgerows and sunlight and joy everywhere. The Bois de

Vincennes! But it's a forest, ivy climbing up the sides of old trunks, green mosses brightening the plaster tones of morbid lichens, thickets becoming bushier and verdure darkening before one's footsteps, suddenly, when one scarcely expected it, throwing up an impenetrable roof and a rampart propitious to timid amours.

Have I told her that I love her? I don't know; and what would be the point? Have our hands and our eyes not betrayed it, in default of our mouths, and do not the glints of joy that radiate in her gaze, and the overflowing and communicative gaiety of her untiring babble, cry out that she knows and that she consents to it, and that she enjoys it, and that she is allowing herself to drift on the azure waves of the beautiful river of amour that is carrying us into I know not what radiant distances? But it can carry us wherever it likes, since we're together . . . !

I have not lived until today. To live is to love. Amour is the Port. Those who love have arrived, the others resemble the busy and feverish bipeds who pace back and forth in railways stations and agitate, breathless, red-faced, stammering, bumping into doors, buzzing like flies around all the windows, bustling and being bustled, jostling and being jostled; they are waiting for the train, they are still waiting, and dying there, in the waiting room, always busy, without having departed.

I love and I live. I live so rapidly and so slowly at the same time that I no longer know what weeks are. It seems to me at the same time that I have always, always known Germaine and that the drama at the lake happened yesterday. She seems to be such an integral part of my life, of my existence, of my needs, of myself, that I cannot do without her for a minute. My *other half.* She really is my other half, in spite of the bourgeois appearance of that expression. I can find nothing that renders my thought better, and the sensation of wellbeing that I experience in her presence, doubled by an indefinable sense of malaise when she draws away by a few feet. If I believed in kabbalistic theories I would say that Germaine is simply—so much is she myself—my own astral body, to which my senses are giving an appearance visible to me alone, and certainly, the distancing of that astral body beyond a certain limit—out of my sight, for example—would be death for me.

The ancient thinkers of Chaldea believed that, in the nebulous origins of humankind, hermaphroditism preceded the separation of the sexes. In all the semitic cosmogonies the first beings were hermaphrodites. Did not Plato say, in the *Symposium*: "Once, human nature was very different from what it is now. In the beginning, there were three species of humans; not two as today, male and female, but a third composed of the two sexes; only the name of that species has remained; it has perished. There was then an androgyne in appearance and name, which united the male and female sex; it no longer exists and its name is an opprobrium. Then, all humans presented a round form; their backs and sides were arranged in a circle, four arms, four legs and two visages supported by a rounded neck, and perfectly similar, a single

166

head uniting those two faces opposed to one another, four ears, two organs of generation, and the rest in the same proportion. The androgynes marched upright, like us, without having any need to turn round in order to take any road they wished. When they wanted to go more rapidly they leaned successively on their eight limbs and advanced rapidly by means of a circular movement, like people turning cartwheels . . . They were redoubtable by virtue of their corporeal strength and their courage, which inspired them with the audacity to climb up to heaven and battle the gods . . . Zeus conferred with the gods as to what to do; they hesitated. The gods did not want to annihilate humans as they had the giants, by striking them dead, because the worship and sacrifices that humans offered to them would have disappeared; on the other hand, they could not suffer such insolence."

Then Zeus, to diminish the strength of humans, split them in two, and Apollo completed the work of the great god by fashioning the belly with the severed skins and articulating the breast with them. In the Babylonian cosmogony of Berossus[1] humans with "two faces and two heads, one male and the other female, on a single body, with both sexes at the

---

1 Berossus was allegedly a Babylonian priest who lived in the fourth century B.C. who wrote a history of Babylon, only known via fragments reported by later Greek writers. One such fragment, describing the deluge in terms similar to those of *Genesis*, was popularized in France in the early nineteenth century, most notably by Marcel de Serres in *De la cosmogonie de Moïse cmparée aux faits géolologiques* (1841). Its authenticity is dubious.

same time" were the beings that preceded present-day humankind.

Human agitation is not devoid of a goal. The generations succeed one another, as feverish and as active; that is because humans, divided by Zeus, can only be happy when complete. They consume their lives searching for their "other halves," which are also searching on their own behalf. When the two souls in pain discover one another, that is Amour, Repose and Quietude. All the rituals of Amour are nothing but symbols: the fusion of the sexes into a unique being, the simulacrum of the reconstitution of the original hermaphrodite. And the sadness consecutive to the act noted by philosophers, who have not sought to explain it—*Omne animal post coitum triste*[1]—stems from the bitter observation of the impotence and inutility of their efforts.

In life, many people are unhappy because they have chosen a partner to whom they are not adapted, who is not their other half but someone else's; and they depart irresistibly upon new searches; hence, adultery. Don Juan searched throughout his life.

Personally, I have not searched, since those presentiments only came to me afterwards. I have found; Germaine is my "soul-sister." We shall die on the same day. Has not the Hand of Coincidence—but coincidences are different and distant effects of the same

---

1 A slight mangling of the beginning of a sentence attributed to Galen, which translates as "all animals are sad after sex [except the cock and the woman]," the origin of the phrase "post-coital tristesse."

invisible cause—already snatched us from the same death, on the same day, at the same place?

She is my Soul-Sister. And we are so completely annihilated in one another, so exactly fused into a single being, one unique Entity, that her speech sometimes responds to my scarcely-formulated thought and her gesture to my unexpressed desire. Our psychologies are intimately and narrowly enlaced, wrapped one around the other; both have nervous anastomoses, adherences of indestructible fibers; between her brain and mine there are endomoses of thoughts, ideas and resolutions, between her heart and mine a flux and reflux of identical sensations, which ensure that our intellectual and moral hermaphroditism is that of the ancient being reconstituted . . .

It is a life that it is impossible to imagine and describe, a life of intellectual delights, of rare sensations, of radiant chastities; for we are still at the prologue of our marvelous poem of amour. Our amour is playing truant in the thickets of Platonism. Why descend from the height of the Dream to wallow in miry Reality? It appears to me that I would no longer be in love. And I want to love, to love, to love forever . . .

VIII

HE has come back. Could such a rare happiness last? Could such a perfect joy and such an absolute tranquility be eternal? I thought for a moment that *Her* coming was going to save me . . . but I had reckoned without my guest. My guest! Oh, yes, my guest, for he inhabits me more and more, infiltrating into my veins and my muscles, into my most tenuous fibers, into the slightest ramifications of my will.

He has returned. I felt him return distinctly. Yesterday morning, I was no longer asleep but I had not yet opened my eyes. My mind was floating in that misty state, in the conscious and languid semi-slumber that I like because of the distance there is between oneself and the external world. Suddenly, I was gripped by an anguish so violent that it seemed to me that I was about to faint, but it was so unlike a faint that my wide-open eyes distinguished perfectly that I was in my bedroom and that I was awake. That sharp pain was so intense that it had provoked a sort of nervous and muscular paralysis, so absolute that for a long time it was impossible for me to move the tip of a finger; my respiration had ceased, large drops of icy sweat were rolling along my temples and I felt that I had been seized again by the frightful Terror of old, the Terror that made the approach of Madness resonate within me drop by drop. And at the same time, I sensed clearly that *He* was taking possession of me again.

(He must be lurking in the solar plexus; it is when he comes out of hiding that the nervous depression is produced that ends in that frightfully suffocating anguish.)

He slid from the solar plexus into the lungs. I felt him; and immediately, the muscles of the thorax came into play, the respiratory anguish disappeared, but the mental anxiety of my true Self was magnified . . .

Well, I'm going mad, that's undeniable, I thought, when I had recovered my calm. *A Being lives within me, inhabits me, which is not me, which has neither my tastes, nor my desires, nor my thoughts.*

Gradually, I recovered my strength. I shook off the torpor that was garotting me and I ran to my mirror . . . Yes, yes, he was really there! He had retaken possession of me. I could no longer doubt it now. *I saw him!* That blue gaze devoid of a pupil, shiny and unquiet, was really his and not mine, those recomposed features, that mouth twisted into an evil rictus, was really him and not me. I did not recognize anything in that face, so changed since the previous day—since he was there—that if I had seen it anywhere but in the mirror of my bedroom I would have mistaken it for the face of another.

And was it not, in fact, the face of another, since it was not mine?

I wanted immediately to corroborate my certainty by means of a decisive experiment. Germaine must be up; I would go and present myself to her . . .

By her attitude, I will see clearly whether the perturbations that have disturbed my physiognomy are as evident as I suppose. I knock on her door, and I call out:

"Knock, knock . . . Germaine! Germaine . . . !"

Damn! Nothing budges, and no one responds . . .

"Germaine! Germaine!"

"Ha ha ha ha!"

It's *Him* who is laughing. Of course! I was quite sure that he was there! He gave no sign of presence, but I sensed within me particular interior somersaults, inexplicable, horribly painful, visceral movements and special contractions of certain muscles ordinarily inert.

But, a singular thing, that laughter, *his* laughter, did not emerge from my throat, nor did I hear it through my ears; I heard it, however, or rather, I perceived it, distinctly. It was, absolutely, an *internal* laughter.

And each vibration of that sarcastic laughter corresponded to a spasmodic contraction of my diaphragm, from which it evidently emanated.

The strangeness and the novelty of the phenomenon confused me momentarily, but the anxiety of wanting to know why Germaine had not responded to me was stronger than my astonishment, and I entered the room abruptly . . .

At the same time as I uttered that "Ah" of astonishment, my diaphragmatic voice, *His* voice, uttered
its strident snigger:

"Ha ha ha ha!"

Not only was Germaine not there—and where
could she be?—but the drawing room had become
the drawing room of old again, which is to say that
the old drawing room had resumed its former physiognomy exactly. Not the slightest trace, not the most
imperceptible vestige, remained of the presence, or
even the passage, of a woman. In the cupboards, in
the furniture, no more dresses, no more fripperies, no
more trinkets . . .

It was as cold as in December and perhaps it was
snowing outside . . . I thought that I was going to die
. . . Bells started to ring within my head and in the
midst of the carillon I heard his voice singing, accom-
panying the buzzing in my ears:

Ha ha ha, you imbecile!
Now you're brought to heel!

"So she had gone! Why? I loved her so much! We
were cooing such a sweet idyll!"

"Ha ha ha!"

"I loved her with a love so tender and so respectful."

"Exactly, imbecile! She wanted something else."

"Wretch!"

"Idiot!"

"Oh, I'll find out where she's gone and go after her."

And I bounded to the staircase.

"I'm going to interrogate the concierge."

"I forbid you to."

"Oh, well, I don't care about your prohibitions."

"We'll see about that."

I ran down the stairs. And as I got closer to the lodge, his voice rose from the diaphragm into the lungs, from the lungs into the bronchi and from the bronchi into the larynx. I felt it rolling like an oppressive and tyrannical ball that vibrated in the taut cords of my exasperated nerves and resonated dolorously. And always this imperious order: "You will say nothing to the concierge."

And I felt the suggestion invade me, gradually dissolving, globule by globule, my whims of revolt; I sensed my will yield in spite of me; and in my thought, instead of the former sentence that I had prepared, I heard another sentence formulated, still very vague, not yet articulated, but already other than the one I willed; a sentence that was already stirring in my tongue and agitating as if to emerge; and when I penetrated into the lodge, I felt that the muscles of my mouth were contracted and outside my influence, and I heard my lips pronouncing, in a hoarse voice that was not mine, the sentence that I had not thought:

"Have you a letter for me?"

In a state of exasperation impossible to relate, I stiffened everything that remained of my Self to cry out in spite of him the other sentence, which I wanted to say, but it was no longer in my memory. It was impossible for me to rediscover it. The contraction of my effort and my rage only succeeded in making me utter an inarticulate cry that appeared to terrify the concierge. I understood that the struggle was impossible and I ran into the street, trembling with fury, rolling murderous projects in my head.

Oh, I'll kill *him*. How, and when? I have no idea; for it's evident that it will be difficult, but I'll think about it . . .

I returned home after a few hours, exhausted by running but a little more settled, my mind calmer, my vision clearer and my perception less obstructed. *He* seemed to have returned to my solar plexus; I was recuperating; the muscles of my tongue, free and supple, worked as I wished; I made sure of that by singing all the way upstairs, and I sang what I wanted.

Will he still only be able to master me momentarily, then?

As I arrived on the fourth floor it seemed to me that I was joyful, as if no worry were buzzing in my head. I climbed that last flight of stairs briskly, my heart a little tense . . . Now I had the certainty of seeing Germaine again. That was impossible, since I was holding the only key to the apartment in my hand, and yet, as I introduced it gently into the lock I heard a voice—Her voice, Germaine's voice—singing the song that I had just been singing while I was climbing the stairs. I pushed the batten of the door violently and I saw her; and I cried, with an indescribable joy:

175

"Germaine!"

She seemed surprised by my joy, and mildly, in her habitual voice, in which the tremolos of an unaccustomed emotion nevertheless vibrated, she said:

"What the matter with you, my friend?"

I succeeded in calming my disturbance and, after a combat of a few seconds, I resolved not to say anything to her, not to ask her for any explanation, in order, in the case that she had not really departed—I am agitating in such a chaos of implausibilities that anything is possible—not to suggest the idea to her. I merely responded:

"Oh, my friend, I love you so much that when I quit you for a few moments it seems to me that Life and Reason withdraw from me.

I did not demand an explanation from myself either. I'm afraid. I no longer want to venture on to the tightrope of analysis. I'm afraid. I went into her room. The former drawing room had lost its sad physiognomy. It had become her bedroom again, cheered up by her trinkets, illuminated by her fripperies. It was warm there, and I respired a mild air, which dilated my lungs.

But why, a little while ago . . . ?

I don't understand; I renounce understanding . . .

I'm scared!

But *She* is here; what does the rest matter?

IX

I'M jealous! Yes, jealous! That's really the word, strange as it may seem and as inexplicable as it might be. It isn't Me whom she loves, it's Him. And I can't complain about it. And if I could, I wouldn't dare, so much do I fear a bitter recrimination that might take her to dire extremities, determine her to flee. I can't complain because today, *He* grips me entirely, he possesses me, he has infiltrated himself in my place, he is annihilating me . . . It's thus that she loves Him, believing that she is loving Me . . .

I can, however, still think. I can even formulate my thoughts in the pages of this journal of my agony, but all speech is forbidden to me.

When I open my mouth, it's his voice that makes heard, with the aid of my larynx, words that I did not want to say. My muscles concur with the gestures he wishes, my legs take him to the places he chooses, and my rage is consumed in impotent whims of revolt, the muscular convulsions of which cannot even be perceived on the surface.

I have thought, no longer being able to speak, of writing to Germaine, in order to reveal to her the trouble in which I am struggling and dying, but would that not frighten her into fleeing? I have renounced the struggle against the Being that invades me, having comr from I know not where, installing his personality, tenacious and invincible, in place of mine. The infiltration is slow, but it is incessant. No muscle of my face belongs to me any longer. I laugh and weep as *he* wishes. The features that my mirror sends back to me and the somber gaze of my eyes are no longer mine. He has cut my beard and shaved my hair in order that the dissemblance should be more striking. He wears colors that I abhor and frock-coats that I abominate; he eats dishes that once sickened me; he gets me up early—me, who adored lying in—and forbids me reading matter that might prop up my poor disjointed intelligence.

Well, when it is him alone who speaks, Germaine listens with voluptuous languors and affections; her beautiful eyes never quit his and their arms interlace.

I'm jealous!

"Oh, how I love you now," she said to him. "In the beginning, you seemed bizarre to me for a long time and I was even a little afraid of you. And then, it's necessary that I tell you, you were a little babyish; your hand scarcely dared hold mine. Today, finally, you're as I desire you to be, and we love one another dearly."

I'm jealous. I witness these gushings impotently. It seems to me that my will is rolling up and convulsing in a paralyzed body. I can no longer forbid these hands, whose muscles are mine and whose gestures are his, certain sacrileges; these lips, he unites with hers at his whim, whereas I would never dare to brush her cheek.

I have understood his goal. Not only does he want to take Germaine from me, but he is seeking to substitute himself for me, to replace my personality with his own, to expel my soul from my body in order to lodge his own therein.

And I sense that he is not far from that result. I observe a change, every morning, an aggravation very difficult to translate. It seems to me that the external world is further away from me. I only perceive it through a semi-transparent veil, which renders objects troubled, shady and tremulous. It is becoming increasingly difficult for me to make a sensation precise, as the means of perception are gradually lacking. By reflecting on it sometimes, I have ended up taking account of my situation. I am simply in the state of an "observer of sensations." I sense them passing, as it were, along the nervous threads, but it is impossible for me to respond to them by a reflexive order. My arm could be placed on a hot stove and I would not suffer from the burn. I would observe tranquilly that I was burning—as if it were someone else—but I could not do anything to withdraw my arm.

I watch myself walking, eating and sleeping, with disinterest. The only thing that is susceptible of provoking my interior ages is the evident amour of Germaine for *him*. I foresee the moment when, vanquished by circumstances, she will give herself to *him* . . . And that day, I sense—and it's perhaps the one thing, the last, of which I'm sure—I shall kill *them*.

The mist that surrounds me is thickening. I can scarcely see to trace these lines, and it costs me a painful effort. The mist is more like a green water in which I am swimming, like a soft gelatin in which I am dissolving, and which penetrates me through all my pores, muffling all sensations to the point that hearing and sight are almost abolished within me.

It seems to me that my soul is falling into deliquescence . . .

It's finished; I'm dispossessed. There are no longer two of us in this wretched body. He is there alone. I am outside. And I perceive, very distinctly, *him*, over there, while I am here; yesterday's mist has dissipated, my sensations have become almost clear again. I say: "I perceive him," and I think "With what eyes?" I say "My sensations are clear," but with what organs am I registering them, since it is him who possesses my organs, since I am floating, at present, in the atmosphere, impalpable and invisible, a mere spirit disengaged from matter, transportable in a second to the other end of the earth. He is *in me*. Him; he has succeeded in expelling me. And it is a relief that I feel in sensing my freedom, disengaged from any material preoccupation, from any link with the external world.

Any link—no! There is a sort of invisible and inexplicable thread that binds me to that body, which I can see at this moment sleeping, over there, on the other side of the room, on my bed, with a placid and gentle play of the muscles of the breast.

I sense that his Being is not necessary to my spiritual life, but that I cannot lose sight of his body. Through that tenuous and fragile thread sensations still pass, very confused, which it would be impossible for me to analyze, but somewhat analogous to those one experiences in a dream when one wants to run in order to escape a danger but it seems to you that you are fleeing with lead boots.

But I have not yet broken off all relation with Him. That relation I shall break. It's necessary that I break it. It's necessary that I kill him, that double thief who has stolen my amour and my body.

But now he's waking up. And getting up. Where is he going? To see Germaine? That illuminated gaze and that shady allure inform me of his intentions . . . He knocks . . . And the soft voice of the Beloved responds without hesitation: "Come in."

In truth, she seems to be waiting for him, her arms open, her mouth moist and smiling, her eyes cheerful.

"Ah, it's you," she says. "What a good awakening."

And the immodest creature does not think about the treacheries of her complicit chemisette, which yawns . . .

"Do you remember the day when you saved me from the most frightful death . . . ? Oh, I no longer want to die, now that we love one another . . ."

They are enlaced, mouth to mouth, breast to breast. And I can no longer hear anything but a confused murmur of kisses and ecstatic sighs . . .

X

I have killed them. They were asleep, exhausted by amour. I have killed them. It was necessary. Her first. Her head, turned toward him, her mouth united with his in slumber, offered a tempting carotid. I cut it with a single stroke of the razor. Her body didn't move, but all her blood flowed out through the gaping wound and soaked the white sheets . . . Gradually, her pink face paled; it became white and livid, and her nose pinched, her eyes opened and the curtain of her eyelids lifted, tugged at the corners by Death . . .

"Ha ha! It's my turn to laugh!"

And I take my time, and don't hurry, for his turn will come—the thief.

His carotid is beautiful, and the bed will slake its thirst . . .

"Ha ha! He who laughs last laughs longest!"

He has just uttered a sigh. Let's go, my beautiful razor, let that sigh be his last. "Ha ha . . . !" Oh, be discreet, my joy, don't wake him . . .

The carotid is beautiful,
The blade will shine;
By its light,
In liberty,
Friends, let's dream . . .

Very gently, very gently, the razor approaches to a millimeter from the artery . . .

And very gently, I lift his eyelid in order to aim my gaze, devoid of an organ, into his eyes one last time.

Ah! I've seen his glaucous eyes! A glimmer has lit up therein, and a terror too . . . Has he seen me, the invisible Me? Has he had a presentiment that I am Dea . . .

Giiiii! The blood has spurted, splashing a red patch on the wall. His eyes, his execrated eyes, rolled in their orbits . . . He's dead . . .

Under the bed I hear, *floc! floc!* . . . Germaine's blood dripping . . .

And now, my turn! Since She is dead, *She*, let's die too, Me! one thrust of the razor and soon there'll be three cadavers here; three cadavers whose blood will drip in the silence, *floc! . . . floc! . . .*

Let's go, *adieu* Life . . . !

THE END OF "THE CONFESSION OF A MADMAN."

EPILOGUE

UNDER the headline *A Mysterious Affair*, this is what was read in the newspapers of the day.

First extract: "The concierge of number 34 Place Daumesnil, on penetrating yesterday into the apartment of one of her tenants, Monsieur D., whose housekeeping she did, found him bathed in a pool of blood. She called for help and sent for a physician, who could only certify the death. The unfortunate had cut his throat with a razor."

Second extract: "We shall return tomorrow to the drama of the Place Daumesnil, which presents bizarre particularities that were not immediately apparent."

Third extract: "We have made a profound investigation of the mysterious affair of the Place Daumesnil and can finally inform our readers fully.

"The suicide is named Marie-Joseph Daucy. He was a young man about thirty years old, of singular appearance but a very tranquil life, living on a pension that he received regularly from a province by registered letter, probably from his family. The concierge was charged with doing his housework and preparing the two meals that he took per day. We have interrogated her and she has been kind enough to give us some information. We shall explain shortly how the documents collected cast a mysterious light on his drama, of which the final word will perhaps never be known. Let us say right away that when the concierge perceived the cadaver it was lying on its back in a pool of blood, the throat agape and a razor between the clenched fingers. According to the legal report, Monsieur Daucy must have killed himself while sitting at a little table on which an abruptly-interrupted manuscript was still open. The last sentence is incomplete. The pen, violently thrown or dropped from the fingers, has made six regular blots on the last page of the manuscript. That manuscript we have been able to procure; it is a veritable novel, but we dare not apply any other epithet to it.

"Let us add nevertheless that the manuscript speaks at length about a certain Germaine who would have lived with Daucy and would have slept in the very room in which the drama occurred. That room, according to the concierge, has always conserved its destination and appearance of a drawing room. It was furnished very simply with a few chairs, some bookshelves and a little square table, the one at which Monsieur Daucy was writing a second before his suicide.

"In the said manuscript, Daucy claims to have murdered the young woman; now, not only was no vestige found of the presence or passage of a young woman in the apartment, but the concierge also affirms categorically that no woman, at any time, ever went into Daucy's apartment. She is all the more competent to make that observation because, I repeat, she had the care of doing her tenant's housework. The murder of Germaine, and her very existence, is thus a pure fiction.

"We say fiction because we are reluctant even to discuss the hypothesis emitted this morning by one of our colleagues, in a serious newspaper that is normally better inspired, which printed the following word for word:

> "*Perhaps the person of Germaine is none other than one of the mysterious beings of which the Reverend Father Louis-Marie Sinistrari d'Ameno speaks in* La Démonialité,[1] *one of those 'reasonable creatures other than human, similarly having a body and a soul, similarly being born and dying, redeemed by Our Lord Jesus Christ and capable of salvation and damnation'* . . . *in a word, a succubus.*

---

1 A French translation of *De Daemonialitate et Incubis et Succubis* by Ludovico Maria Sinistrari (1622-1701), a Franciscan teacher of philosophy and theology and an advisor to the Inquisition in Rome. The text was one of several by Sinistrari examining supposed human intercourse with demons as well as other sexual sins, which listed in passing the effects of various psychotropic substances employed in attempts to exorcise demons. A general work he compiled on criminology and penology, commissioned by his Order, was placed on the Index of prohibited books by the College of Cardinals, for unspecified reasons.

187

"We admit for our count that we prefer the explanation by means of hallucination—a complex hallucination, it is true, requiring the collaboration of all the senses—to the explanation by means of a succubus, an explanation perhaps orthodox, but assuredly unscientific.

"Marie-Joseph Daucy, still according to the information given by the concierge, was eccentric; he often talked to himself and he had singular manias, which she had always respected. On the day when she entered into his service he had said to her, after having explained what she had to do: 'I must warn you that I detest chatter. Perform your service therefore, without saying a word to me. I have manias, respect them without discussion.' She had obeyed. It was thus that he instructed her one day to set two places at table because someone—a woman—would be eating with him henceforth. Well, that woman had never appeared; and yet, whenever her place-setting was forgotten, he pointed it out to her. Sometimes his gaze frightened her; the expression of his visage changed, he no longer looked the same. What is more, he appeared to perceive that, and went, on those days, to look to himself in the mirror. There, he waved his fist at his image and shouted, while contracting his mouth: 'Swine! Swine! Swine!'

"On the eve of his death, he seemed even more bizarre than usual. He was sad, absorbed and ate very little. She asked him several times if he was ill, but he did not appear to hear. Furthermore, it had been a full fortnight since, according to the good woman's expression, 'it had all started.' His habits had altered completely. He no longer went out, got up early, having previously stayed in bed until eleven o'clock, and asked her for his meals precisely what he had previously declared that he could not abide.

"On the other hand, very sober to begin with, in those final days he consumed an immoderate amount of cognac, and the local pharmacist admitted that in the course of more than a month he had delivered a frightful quantity of morphine to him. Perhaps that ought to be seen as the explanation of the complex hallucination that he humanized under the name of Germaine.

"Finally, according to the manuscript, Monsieur Daucy had been living in his apartment for approximately two years, and the concierge affirmed to us that he had only been accommodated there for six months.

"In brief, we admit our impotence to elucidate whether we are in the presence of a hoaxer or a madman."

A PARTIAL LIST OF SNUGGLY BOOKS